EVER LOVIN' Marmaduke

by Brad Anderson

A TOM DOHERTY ASSOCIATES BOOK
NEW YORK

This is a work of fiction. All the characters and events portrayed in this book are fictional, and any resemblance to real people or incidents is purely coincidental.

EVER LOVIN' MARMADUKE

Copyright © 1985 by United Feature Syndicate, Inc.

Marmaduke comic strips copyright © 1976, 1977, 1980, 1981 and 1983 by United Feature Syndicate, Inc.

All rights reserved, including the right to reproduce this book, or portions thereof, in any form.

A Tor Book
Published by Tom Doherty Associates, Inc.
49 West 24th Street
New York, N.Y. 10010

ISBN: 0-812-51017-8

First edition: August 1990

Printed in the United States of America

0 9 8 7 6 5 4 3 2 1

Ever Lovin' Marmaduke

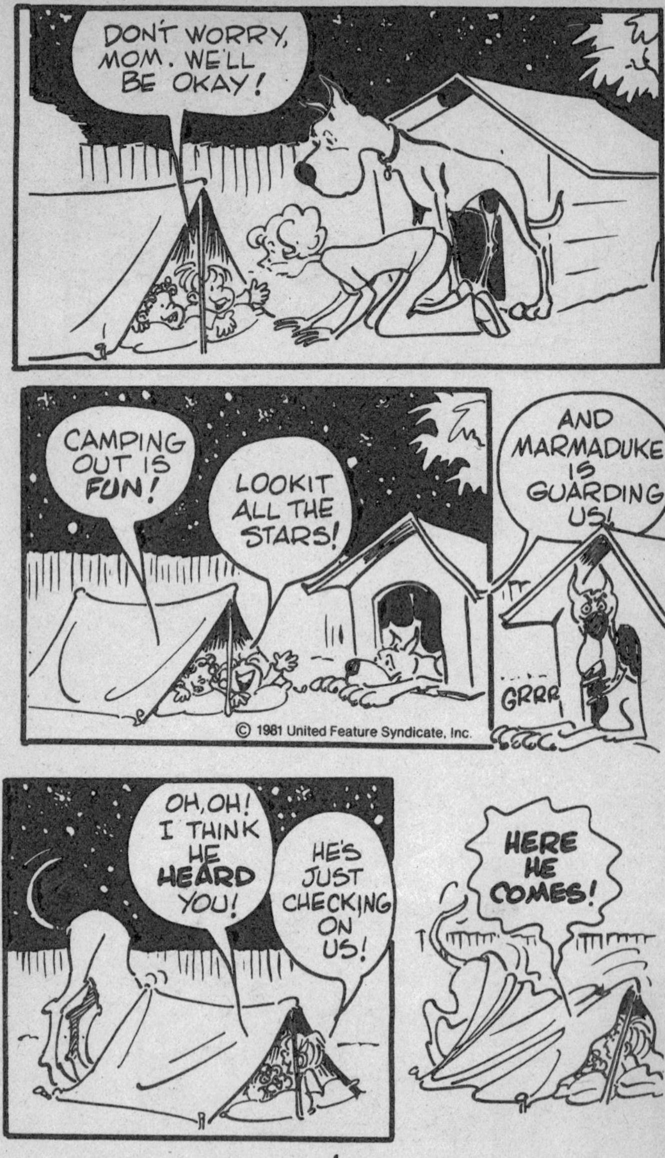
DON'T WORRY, MOM. WE'LL BE OKAY!
CAMPING OUT IS **FUN**!
LOOKIT ALL THE STARS!
© 1981 United Feature Syndicate, Inc.
AND MARMADUKE IS GUARDING US!
GRRR
OH, OH! I THINK HE **HEARD** YOU!
HE'S JUST CHECKING ON US!
HERE HE COMES!

MARMADUKE! GET OUTA HERE!
SLURP!
6·21
ARE WE STILL CAMPING OUT?
BRAD ANDERSON

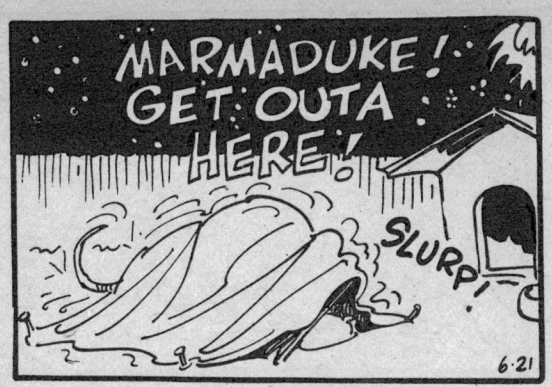

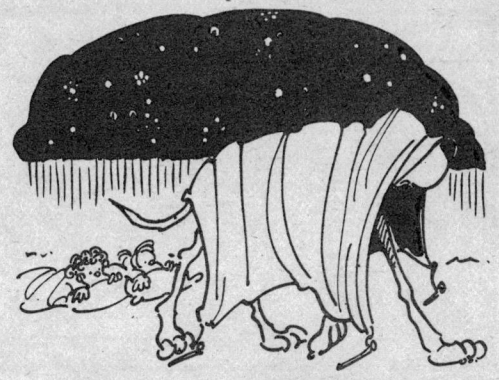

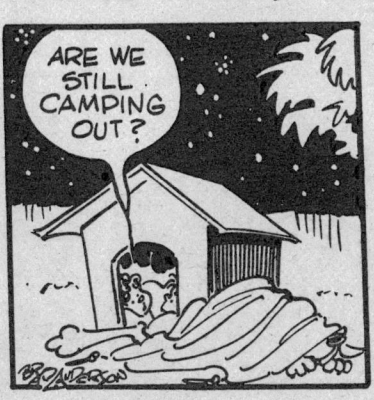

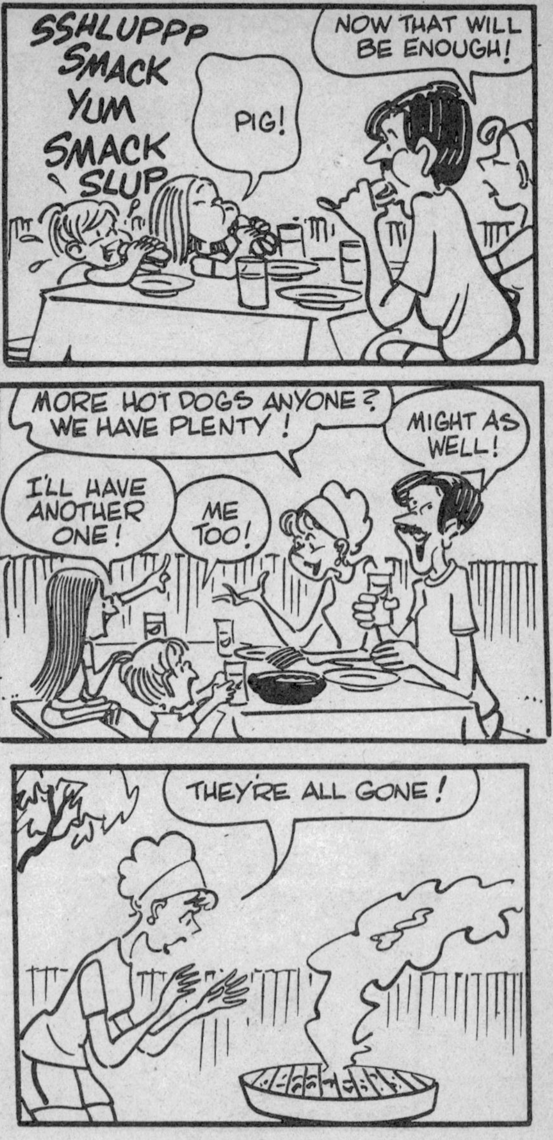
SSHLUPPP SMACK YUM SMACK SLUP
PIG!
NOW THAT WILL BE ENOUGH!
MORE HOT DOGS ANYONE? WE HAVE PLENTY!
MIGHT AS WELL!
I'LL HAVE ANOTHER ONE!
ME TOO!
THEY'RE ALL GONE!

THEY CAN'T BE!
I ONLY HAD ONE!
ME TOO!
I HAD...er... TWO!
AND I HAD TWO...
THAT LEAVES SIX UNACCOUNTED FOR...
BURP
6-28
THEY'RE ACCOUNTED FOR!
MARMADUKE!
BURP
© 1981 United Feature Syndicate, Inc.
BRAD ANDERSON

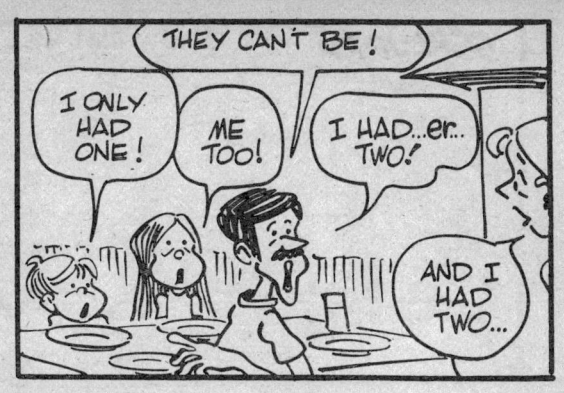

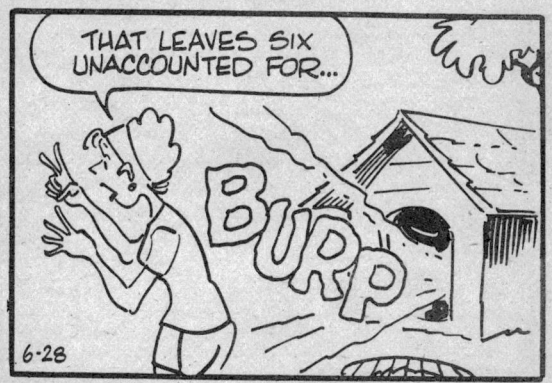

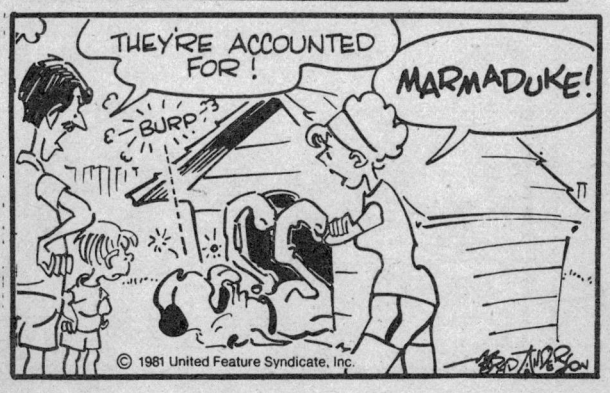

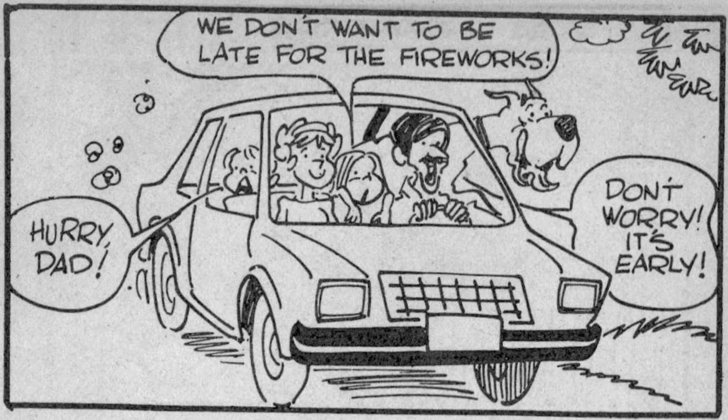
WE DON'T WANT TO BE LATE FOR THE FIREWORKS!
HURRY, DAD!
DON'T WORRY! IT'S EARLY!

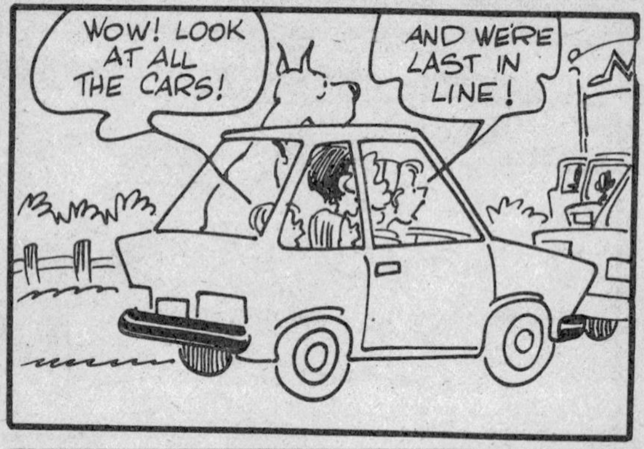
WOW! LOOK AT ALL THE CARS!
AND WE'RE LAST IN LINE!

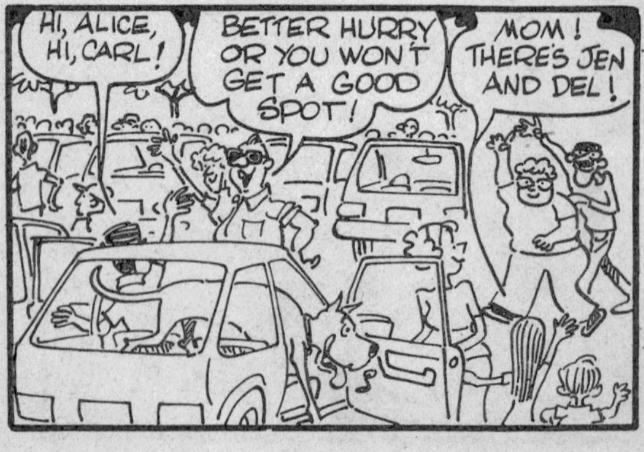
HI, ALICE, HI, CARL!
BETTER HURRY OR YOU WON'T GET A GOOD SPOT!
MOM! THERE'S JEN AND DEL!

I CAN'T SEE!
ME, NEITHER!
7-5
WOOF WOOF WOOF WOOF WOOF WOOF
BOOM
YEP! THANKS TO GOOD OL' MARMADUKE
FOOF
FOOF
BOOM
WOW! WE GOT THE BEST SPOT IN THE WHOLE PARK.

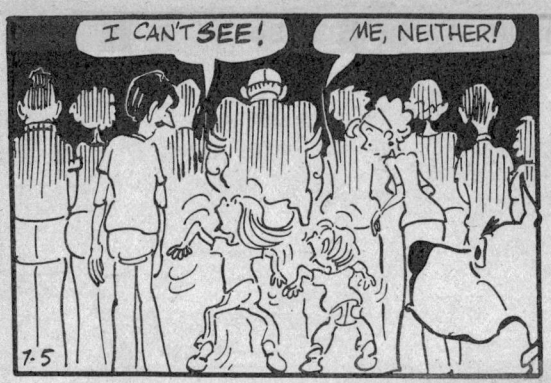

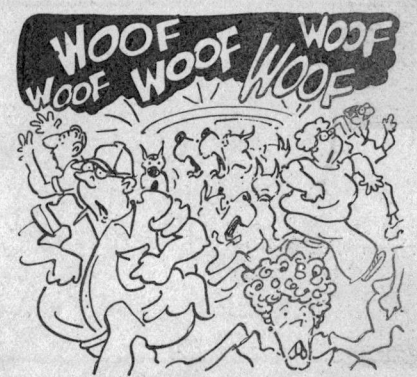

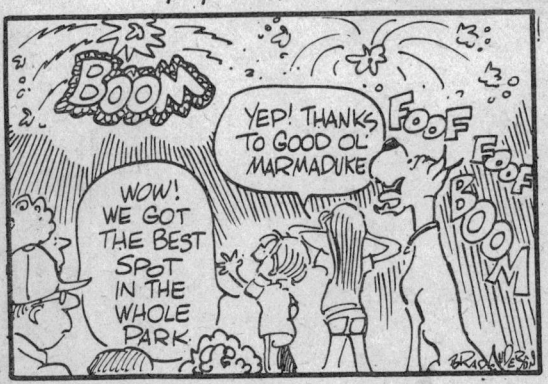

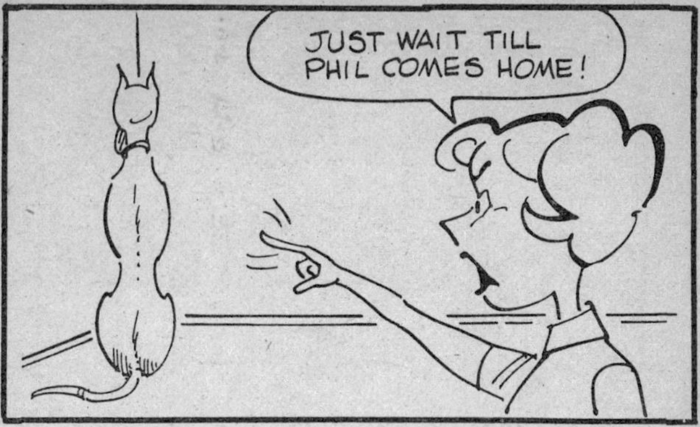
JUST WAIT TILL PHIL COMES HOME!

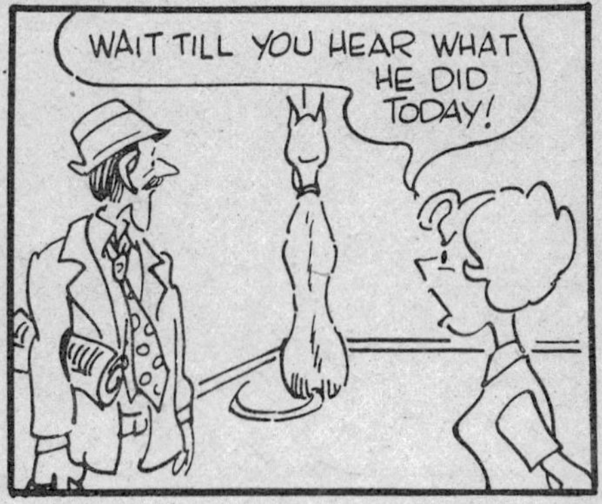
WAIT TILL YOU HEAR WHAT HE DID TODAY!

HE KNOCKED OVER A GOOD LAMP!

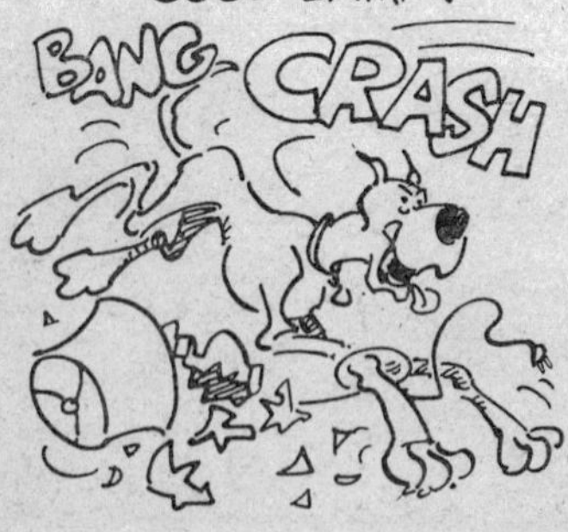
BANG
CRASH

HE TRACKED MUD ALL OVER MY CLEAN KITCHEN FLOOR!

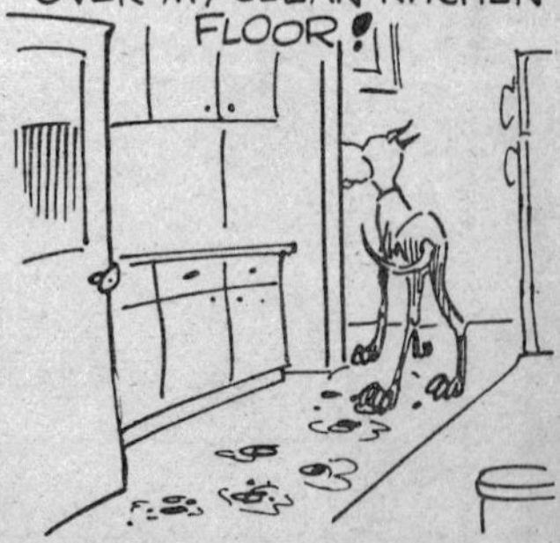

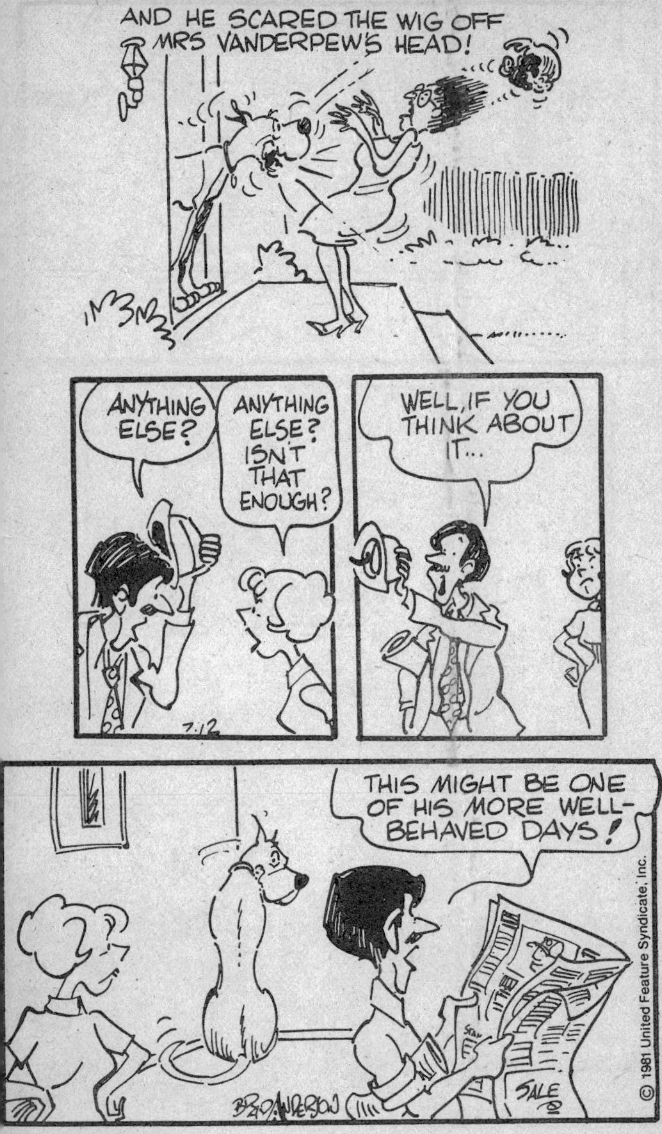
AND HE SCARED THE WIG OFF MRS VANDERPEW'S HEAD!
ANYTHING ELSE?
ANYTHING ELSE? ISN'T THAT ENOUGH?
WELL, IF YOU THINK ABOUT IT...
THIS MIGHT BE ONE OF HIS MORE WELL-BEHAVED DAYS!

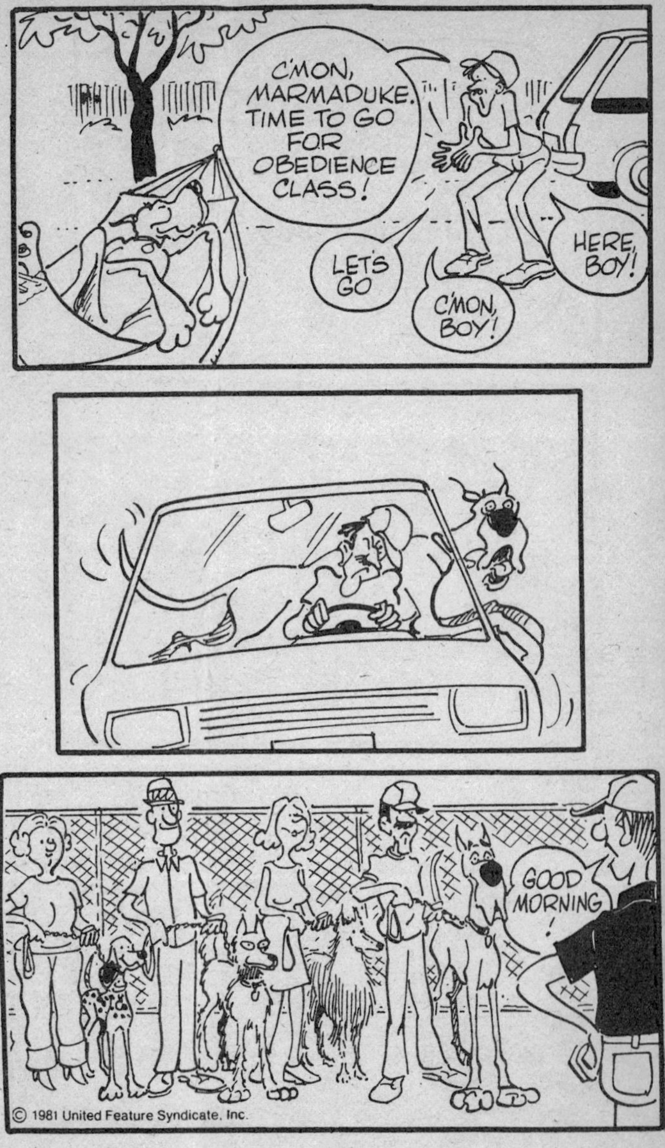
C'MON, MARMADUKE. TIME TO GO FOR OBEDIENCE CLASS!
LET'S GO
C'MON, BOY!
HERE, BOY!
GOOD MORNING!

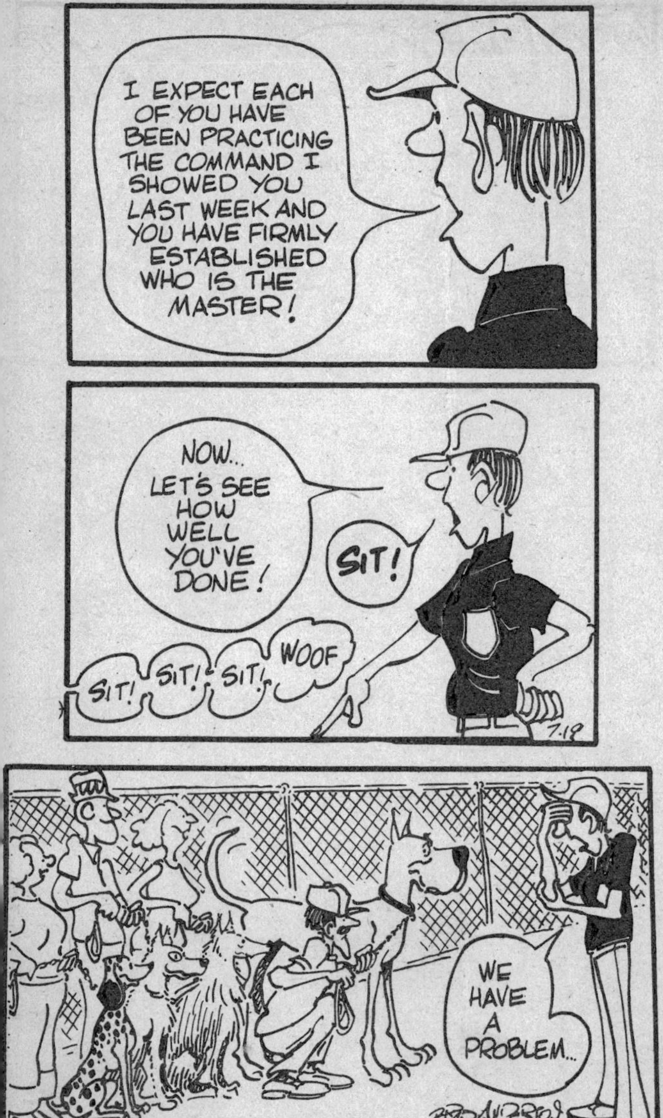
I EXPECT EACH OF YOU HAVE BEEN PRACTICING THE COMMAND I SHOWED YOU LAST WEEK AND YOU HAVE FIRMLY ESTABLISHED WHO IS THE MASTER!
NOW... LET'S SEE HOW WELL YOU'VE DONE!
SIT!
SIT!
SIT!
SIT!
WOOF
WE HAVE A PROBLEM...

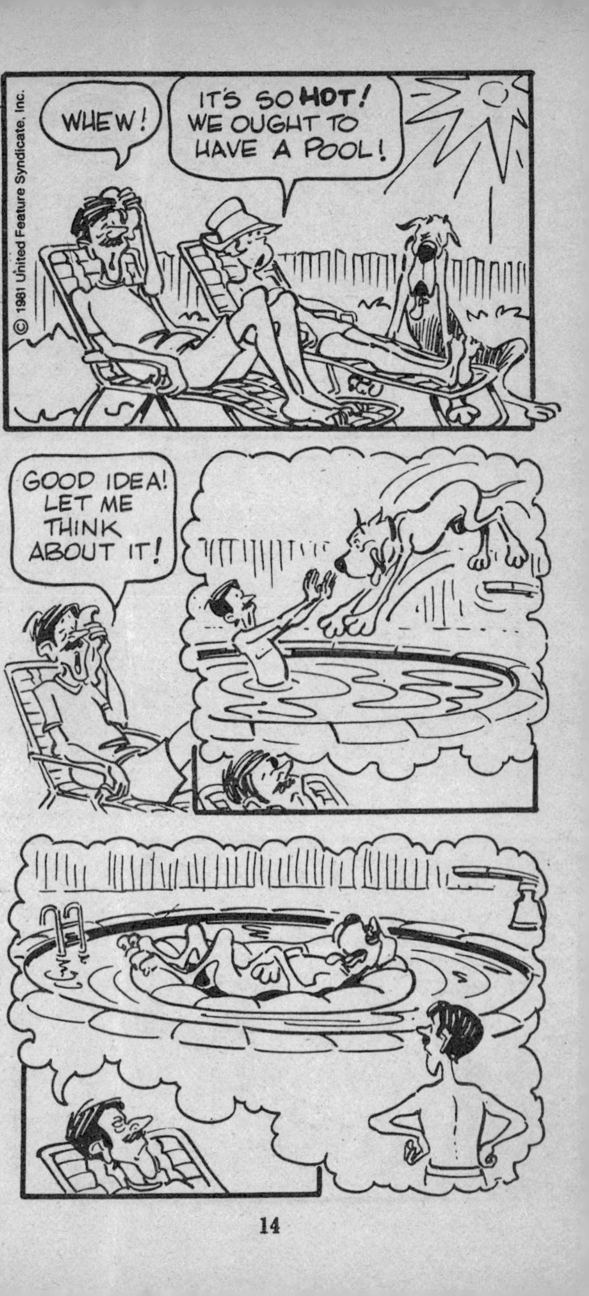
© 1981 United Feature Syndicate, Inc.
WHEW!
IT'S SO HOT! WE OUGHT TO HAVE A POOL!
GOOD IDEA! LET ME THINK ABOUT IT!

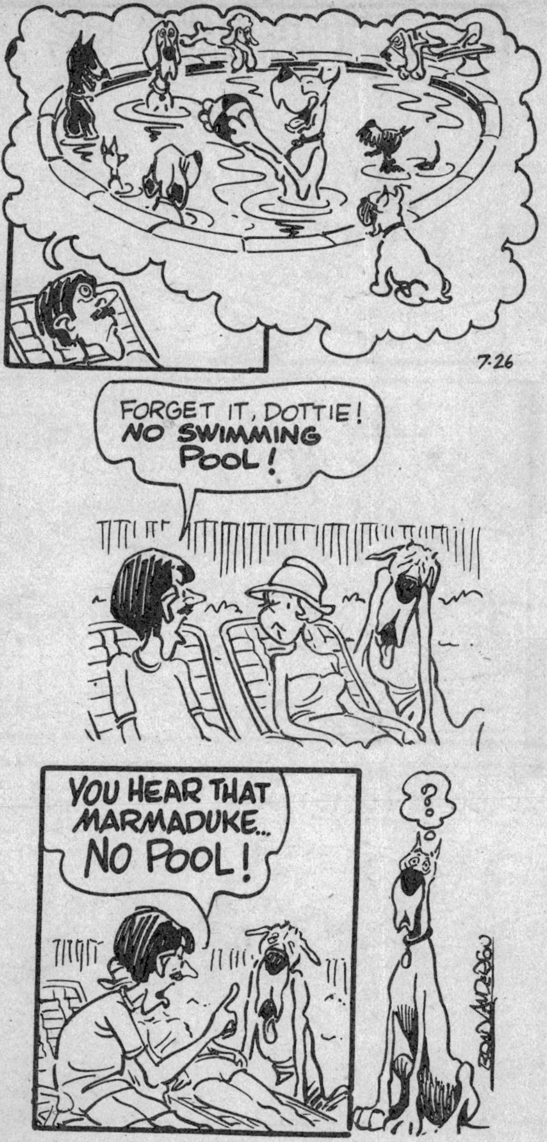
7·26
FORGET IT, DOTTIE! NO SWIMMING POOL!
YOU HEAR THAT MARMADUKE... NO POOL!
?
BRAD ANDERSON

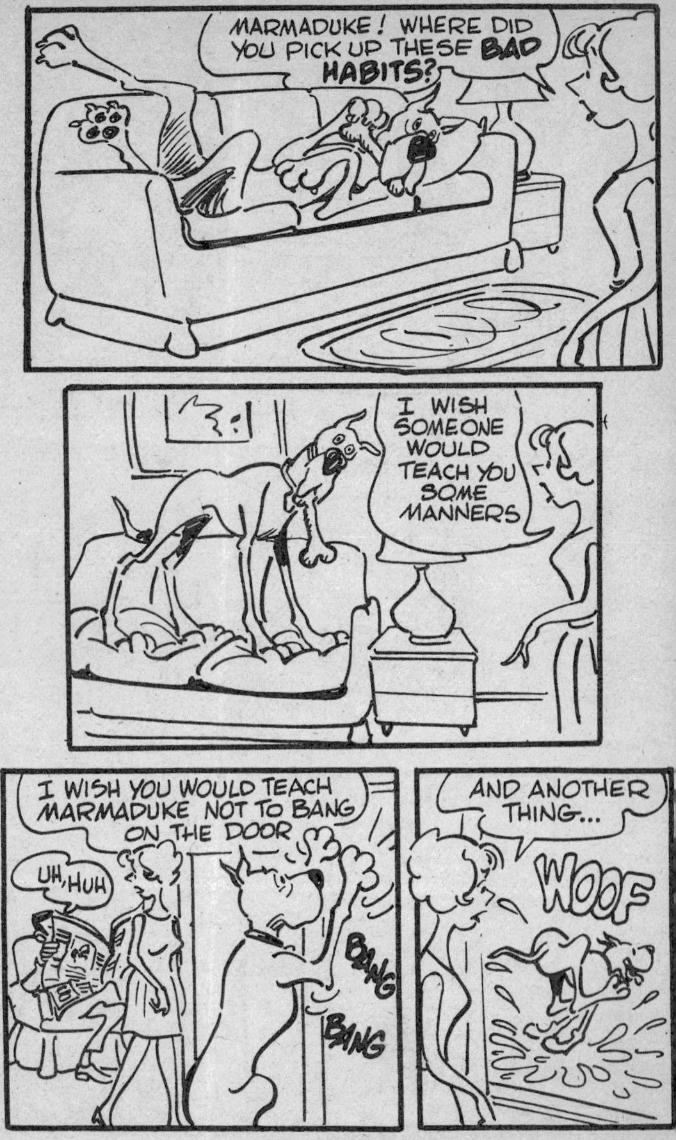
MARMADUKE! WHERE DID YOU PICK UP THESE BAD HABITS?
I WISH SOMEONE WOULD TEACH YOU SOME MANNERS
I WISH YOU WOULD TEACH MARMADUKE NOT TO BANG ON THE DOOR
UH, HUH
BANG
BANG
AND ANOTHER THING...
WOOF

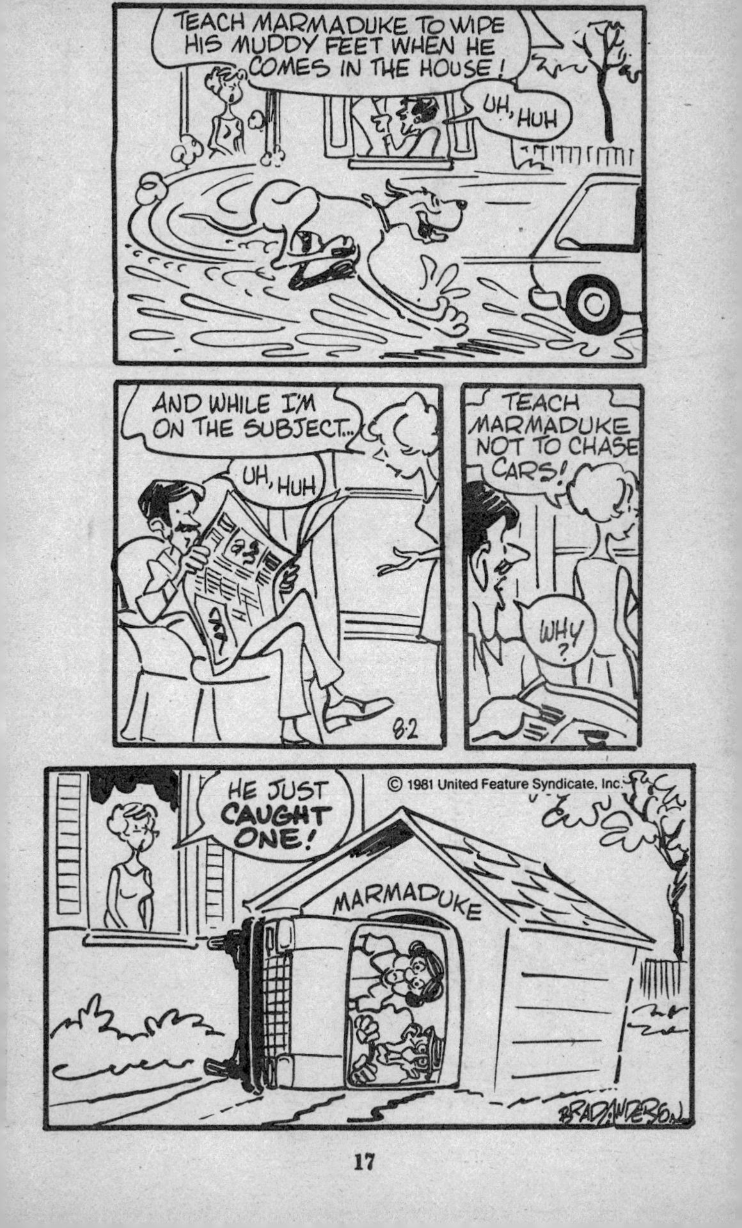
TEACH MARMADUKE TO WIPE HIS MUDDY FEET WHEN HE COMES IN THE HOUSE!
UH, HUH
AND WHILE I'M ON THE SUBJECT...
UH, HUH
8-2
TEACH MARMADUKE NOT TO CHASE CARS!
WHY?
© 1981 United Feature Syndicate, Inc.
HE JUST CAUGHT ONE!
MARMADUKE
BRAD ANDERSON

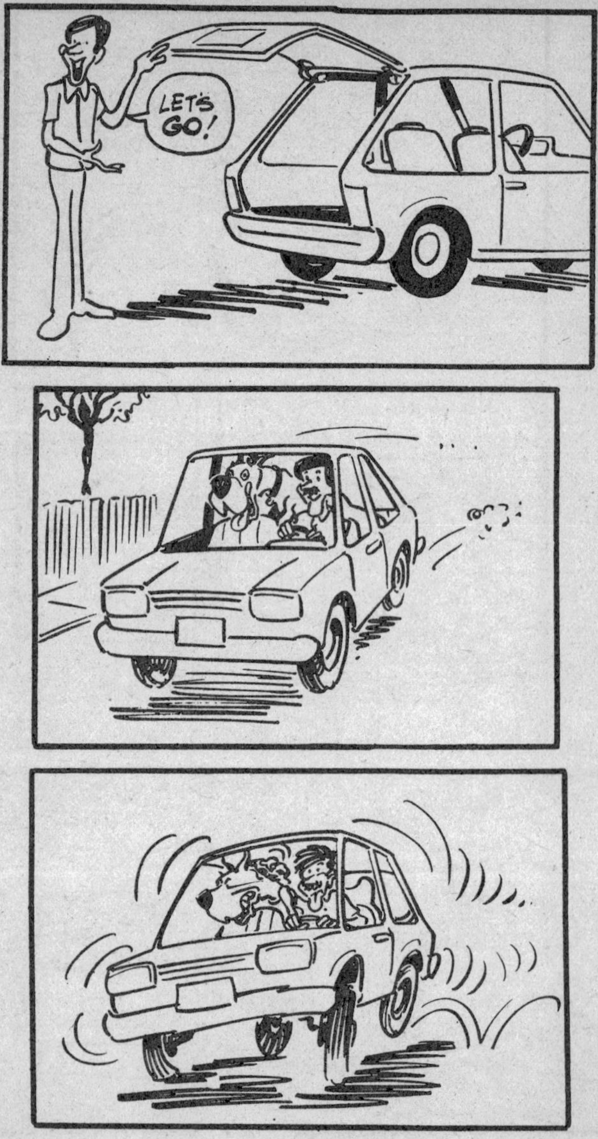
LET'S GO!

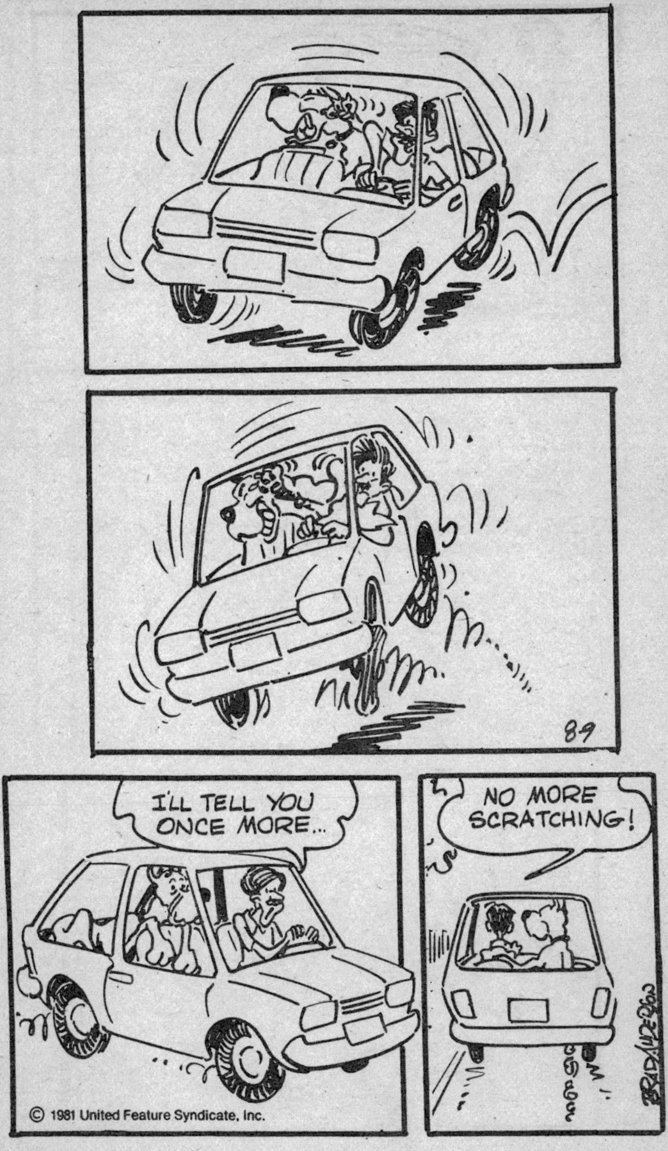
I'LL TELL YOU ONCE MORE...
NO MORE SCRATCHING!

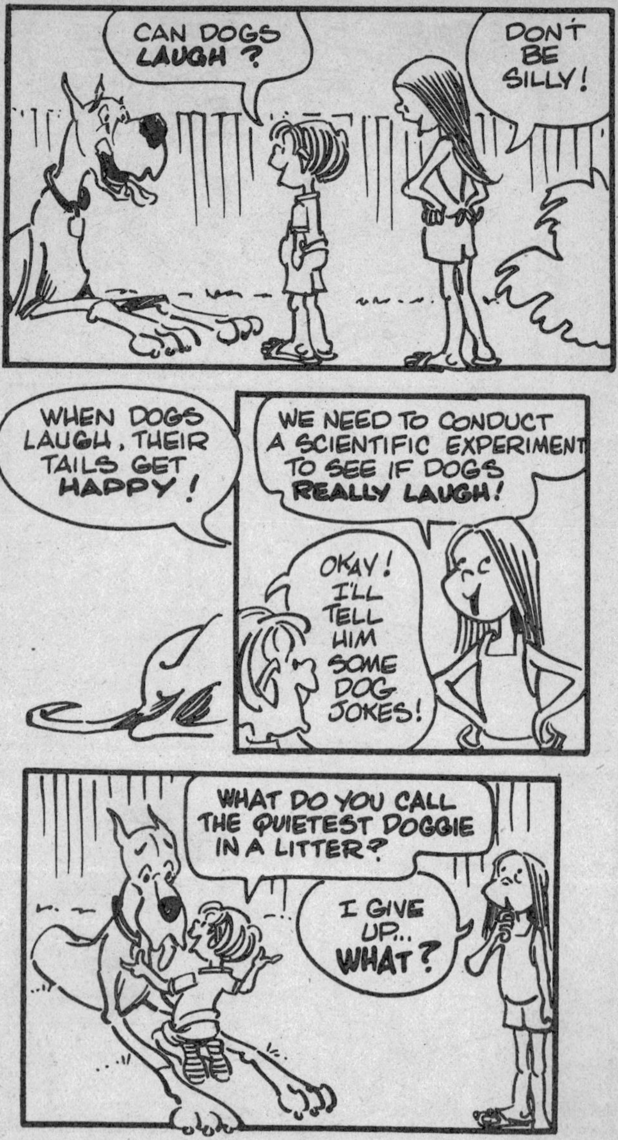
CAN DOGS LAUGH ?
DON'T BE SILLY!
WHEN DOGS LAUGH, THEIR TAILS GET HAPPY!
WE NEED TO CONDUCT A SCIENTIFIC EXPERIMENT TO SEE IF DOGS REALLY LAUGH!
OKAY! I'LL TELL HIM SOME DOG JOKES!
WHAT DO YOU CALL THE QUIETEST DOGGIE IN A LITTER?
I GIVE UP... WHAT?

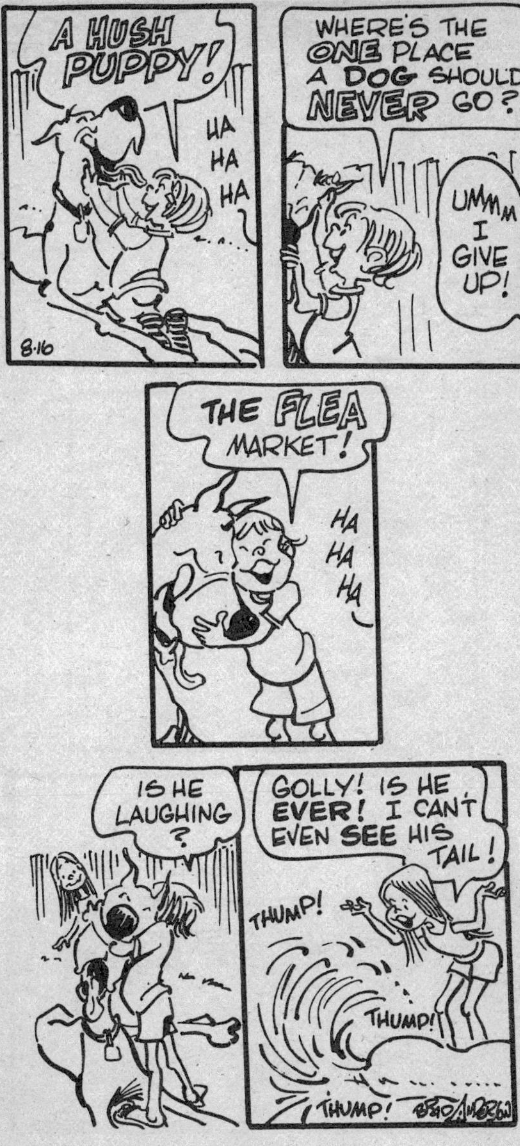
A HUSH PUPPY!
HA HA HA
8·16
WHERE'S THE ONE PLACE A DOG SHOULD NEVER GO?
UMMM I GIVE UP!
THE FLEA MARKET!
HA HA HA
IS HE LAUGHING?
GOLLY! IS HE EVER! I CAN'T EVEN SEE HIS TAIL!
THUMP!
THUMP!
THUMP!

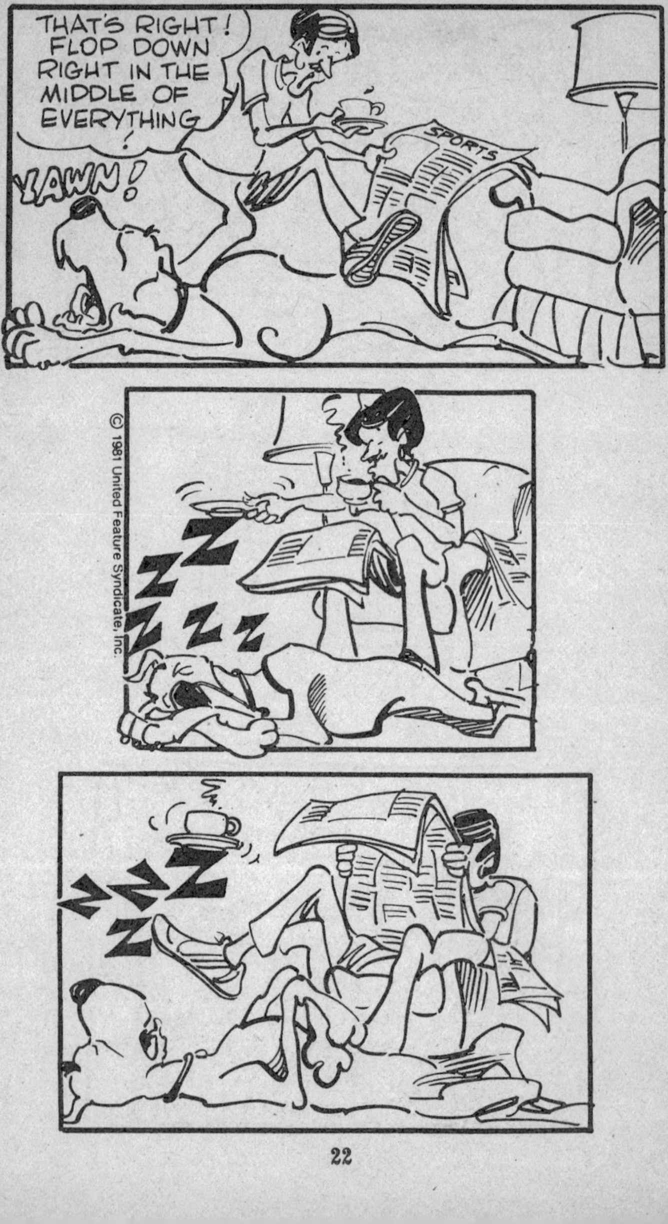
THAT'S RIGHT! FLOP DOWN RIGHT IN THE MIDDLE OF EVERYTHING?
YAWN!
SPORTS

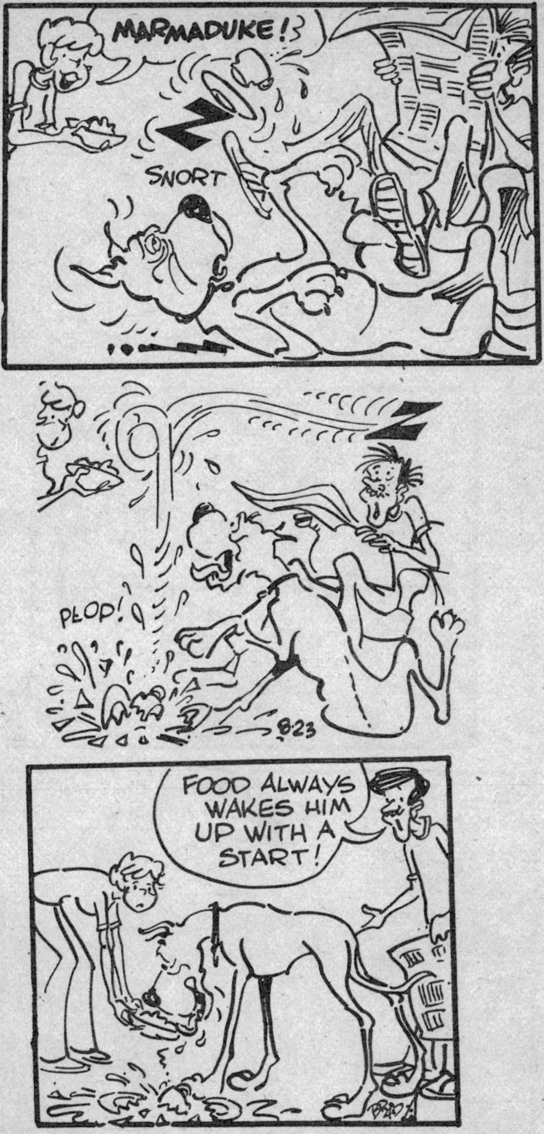
MARMADUKE!
SNORT
PLOP!
8·23
FOOD ALWAYS WAKES HIM UP WITH A START!

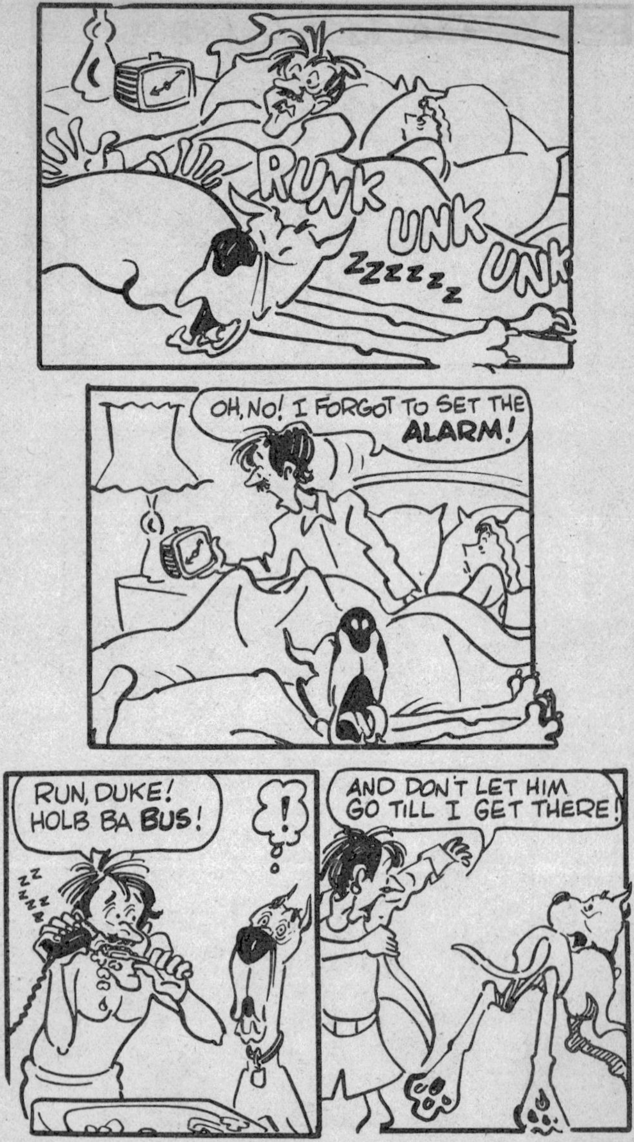
RUNK
UNK
UNK
ZZZZZZZ
OH, NO! I FORGOT TO SET THE ALARM!
RUN, DUKE! HOLB BA BUS!
!
AND DON'T LET HIM GO TILL I GET THERE!

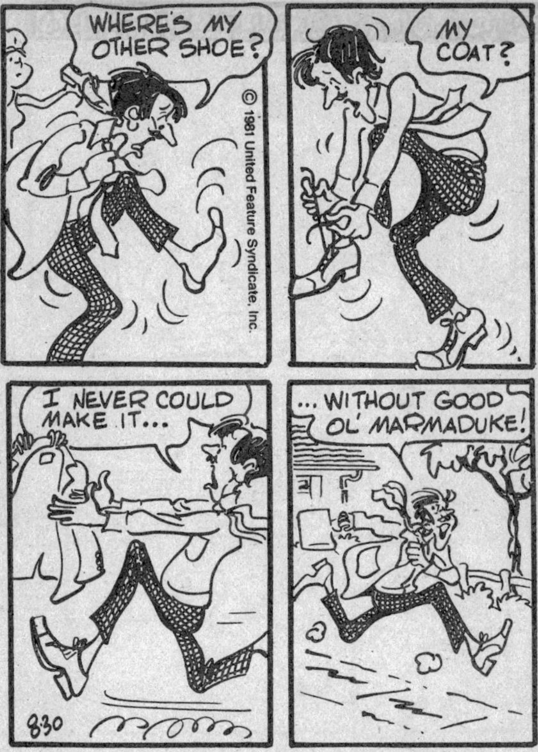
WHERE'S MY OTHER SHOE?
© 1981 United Feature Syndicate, Inc.
MY COAT?
I NEVER COULD MAKE IT...
830
... WITHOUT GOOD OL' MARMADUKE!

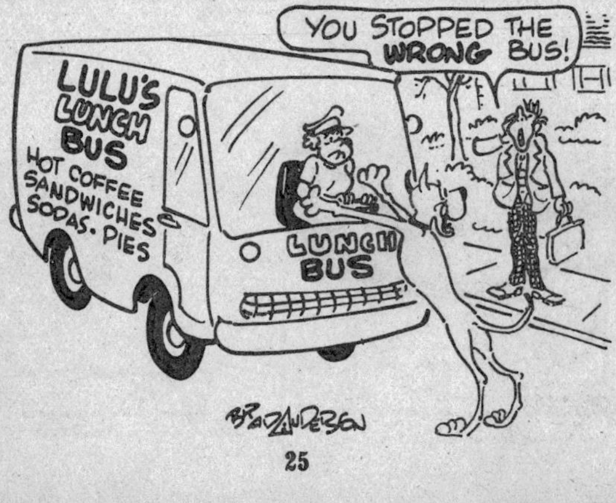
YOU STOPPED THE WRONG BUS!
LULU'S LUNCH BUS
HOT COFFEE SANDWICHES SODAS. PIES
LUNCH BUS

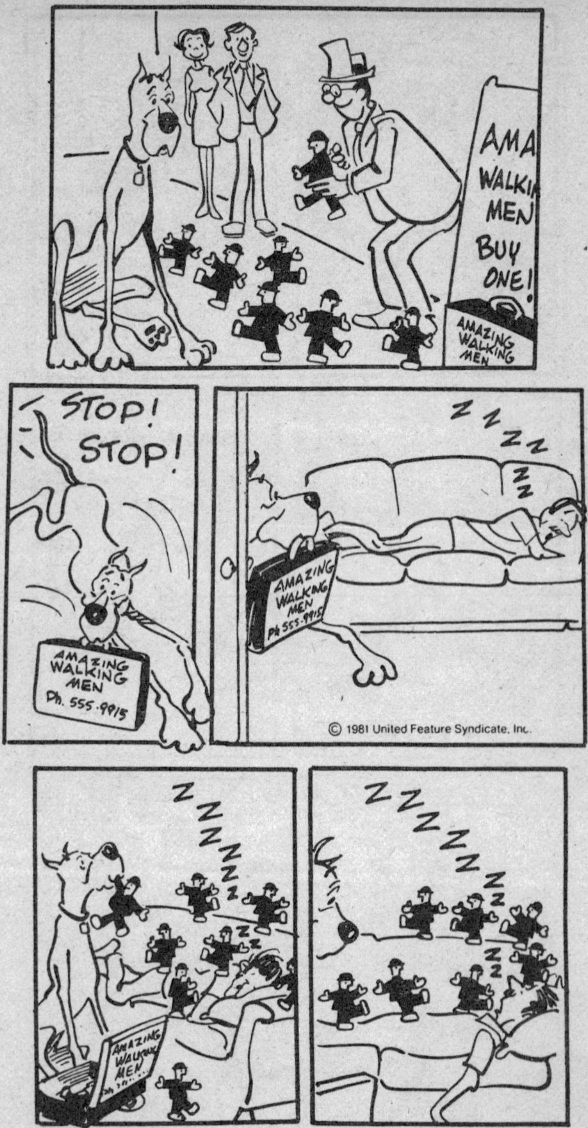
AMA
WALKI
MEN
BUY ONE!
AMAZING WALKING MEN
STOP! STOP!
AMAZING WALKING MEN Ph. 555-9915
ZZZZ
AMAZING WALKING MEN Ph 555-9915
ZZZZ
AMAZING WALKING MEN
ZZZZZ

ZZZ
AMAZING WALKING MEN Ph 555-9915
ZZZZZ
I JUST HAD THE MOST HORRIBLE NIGHTMARE!
LITTLE MEN MARCHING ALL OVER ME!
AFTER YOU PULL YOURSELF TOGETHER YOU HAVE A PHONE CALL TO MAKE!
AMAZING WALKING MEN Ph. 555-9915
BRAD ANDERSON
9-6

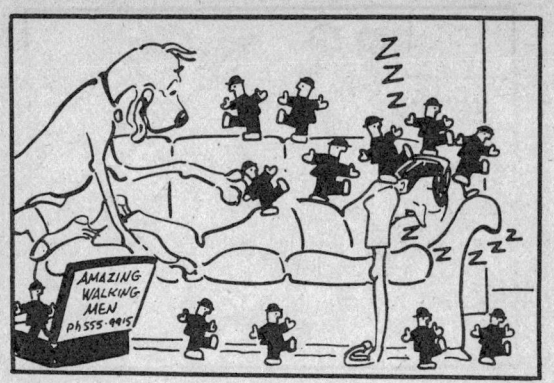

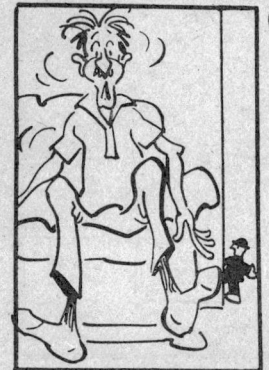

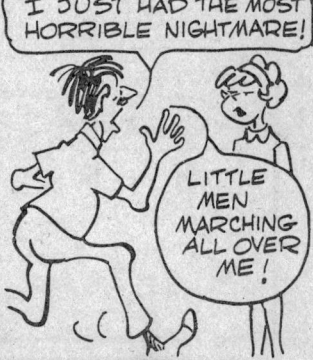

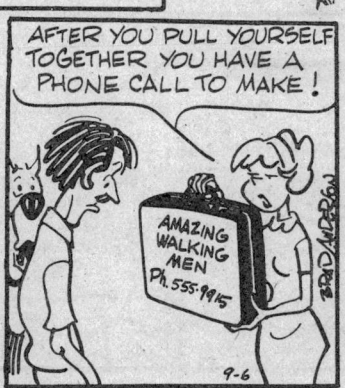

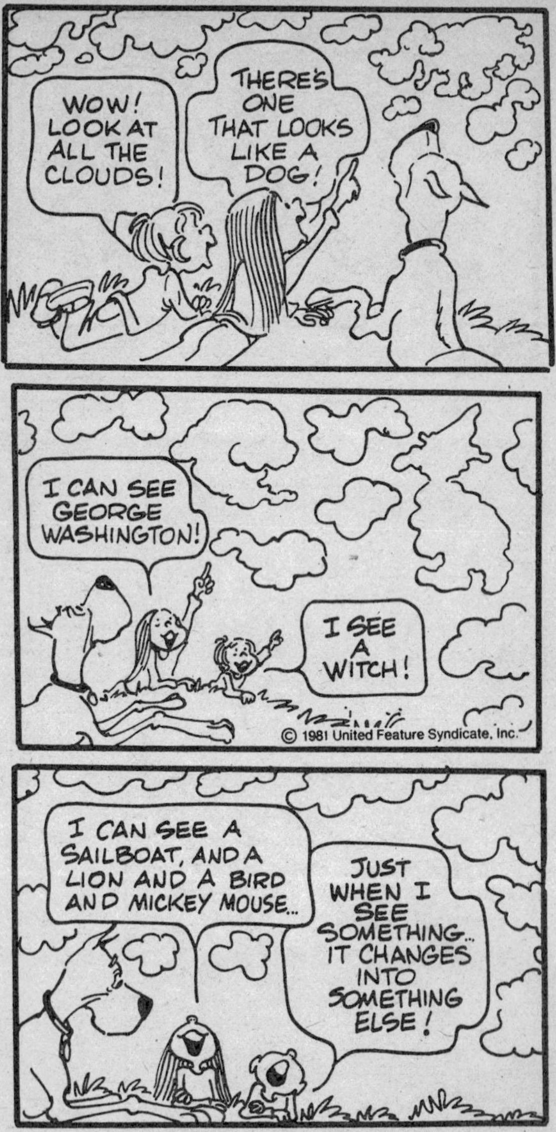
WOW! LOOK AT ALL THE CLOUDS!
THERE'S ONE THAT LOOKS LIKE A DOG!
I CAN SEE GEORGE WASHINGTON!
I SEE A WITCH!
© 1981 United Feature Syndicate, Inc.
I CAN SEE A SAILBOAT, AND A LION AND A BIRD AND MICKEY MOUSE...
JUST WHEN I SEE SOMETHING... IT CHANGES INTO SOMETHING ELSE!

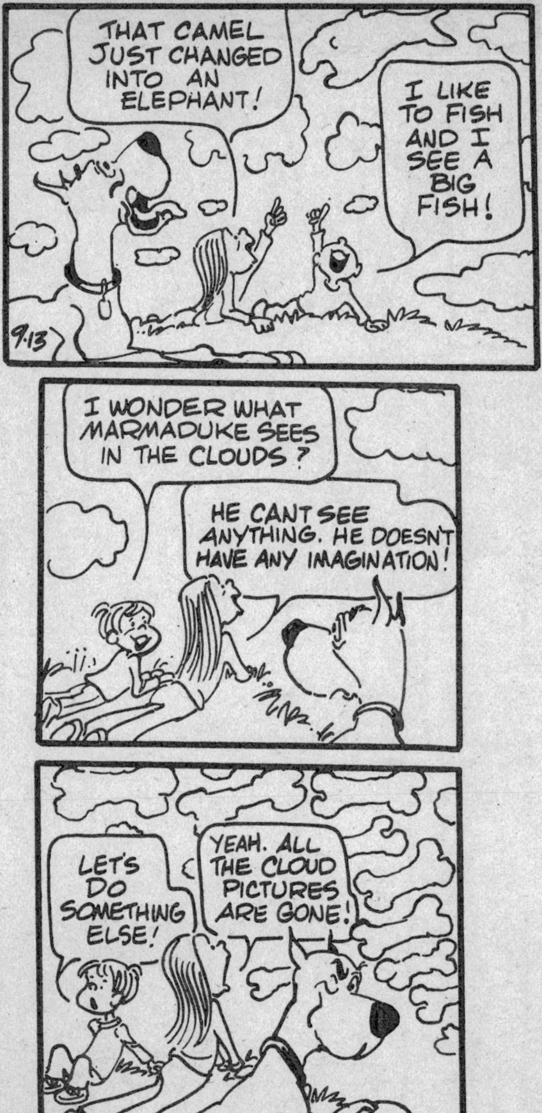
THAT CAMEL JUST CHANGED INTO AN ELEPHANT!
I LIKE TO FISH AND I SEE A BIG FISH!
9.13
I WONDER WHAT MARMADUKE SEES IN THE CLOUDS?
HE CANT SEE ANYTHING. HE DOESN'T HAVE ANY IMAGINATION!
LET'S DO SOMETHING ELSE!
YEAH. ALL THE CLOUD PICTURES ARE GONE!

NO! I DON'T WANT TO GO FOR A WALK!
CLUNK CLUNK
GO AWAY!

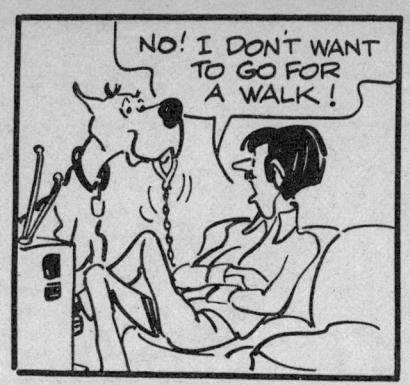

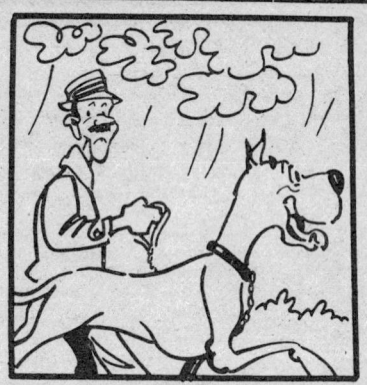

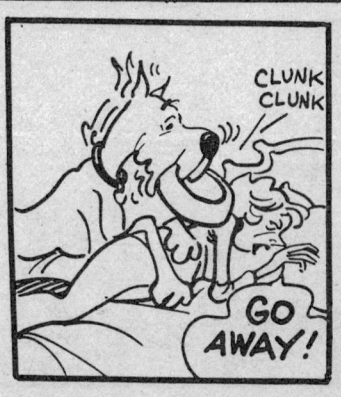

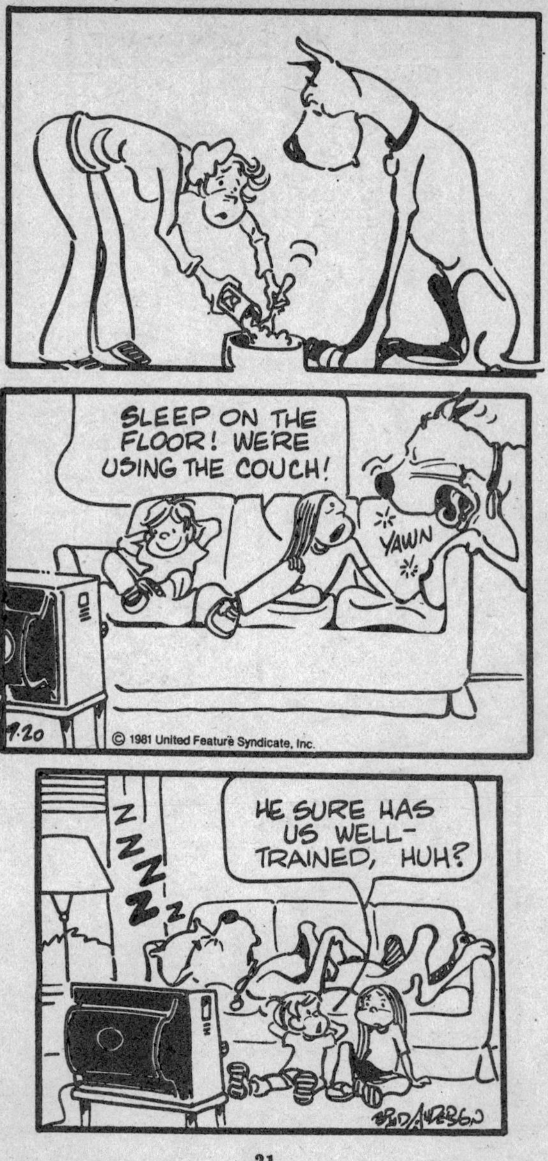
SLEEP ON THE FLOOR! WE'RE USING THE COUCH!
YAWN
9·20
© 1981 United Feature Syndicate, Inc.
Z Z Z Z z
HE SURE HAS US WELL-TRAINED, HUH?

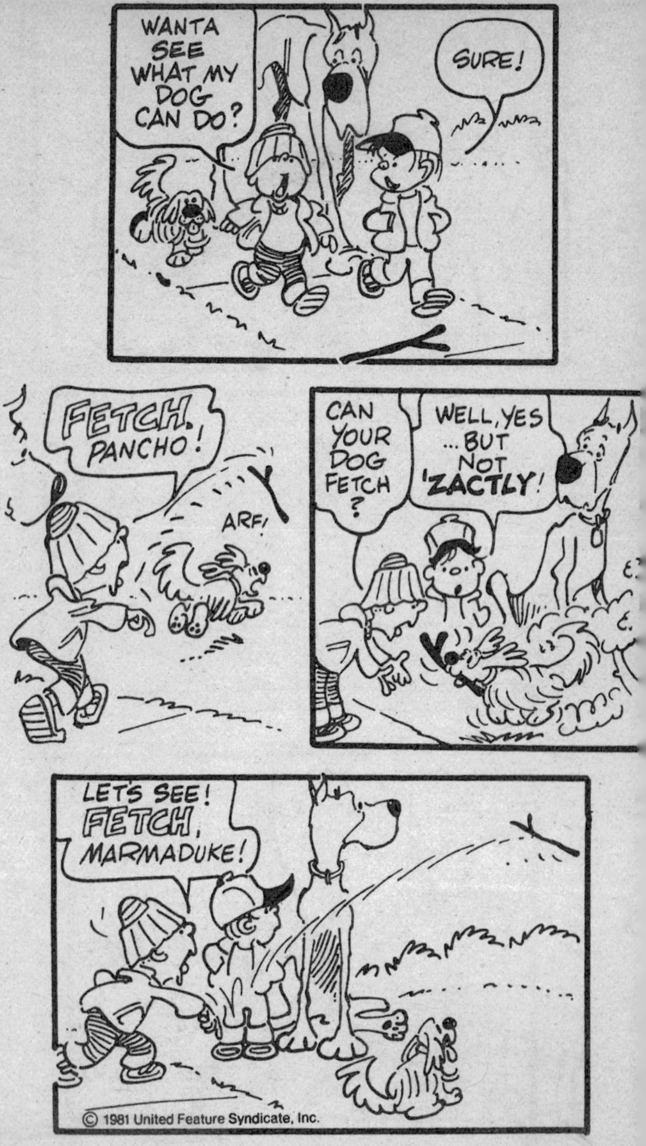
WANTA SEE WHAT MY DOG CAN DO?
SURE!
FETCH, PANCHO!
ARF!
CAN YOUR DOG FETCH?
WELL, YES ... BUT NOT 'ZACTLY!
LETS SEE! FETCH, MARMADUKE!

WOOF
9·27
HE BOSSES!

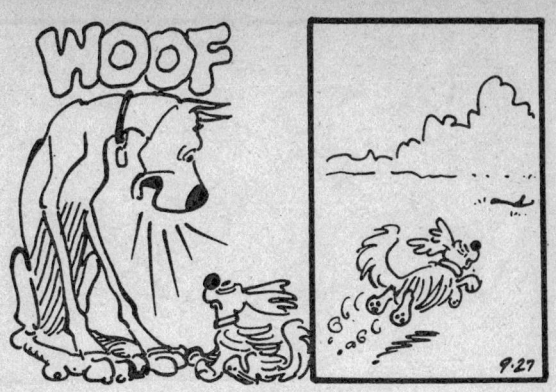

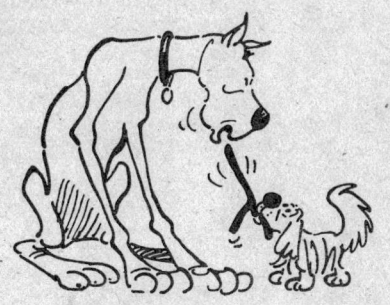

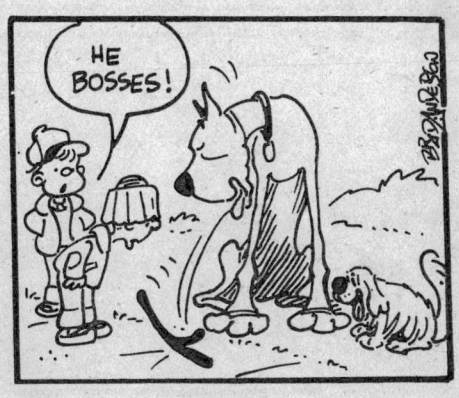

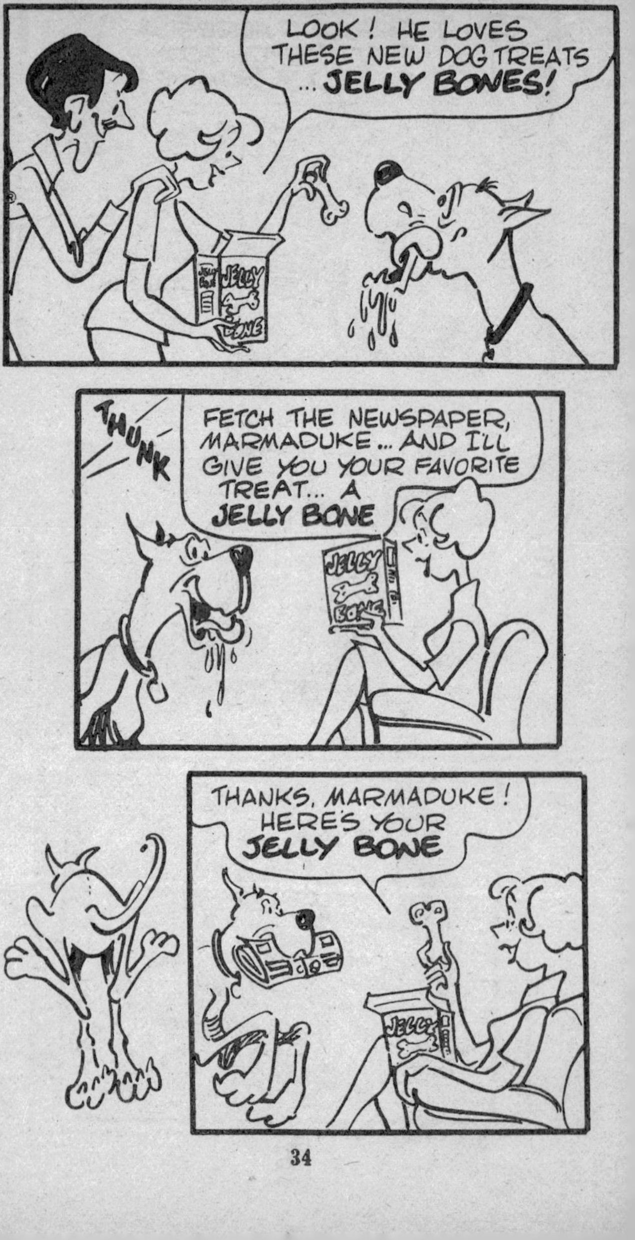
LOOK! HE LOVES THESE NEW DOG TREATS ... JELLY BONES!
THUNK
FETCH THE NEWSPAPER, MARMADUKE ... AND I'LL GIVE YOU YOUR FAVORITE TREAT... A JELLY BONE
THANKS, MARMADUKE! HERE'S YOUR JELLY BONE

OH, GOOD! HERE'S A FREE COUPON FOR JELLY BONES!
NEW DOG TREAT JELLY BONES
FREE
FOOD
10·4
HEY! THAT'S MY PAPER!

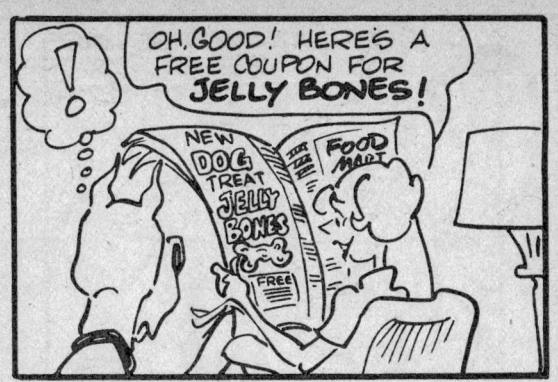

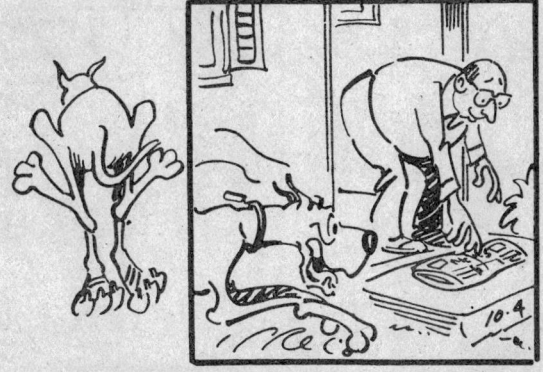

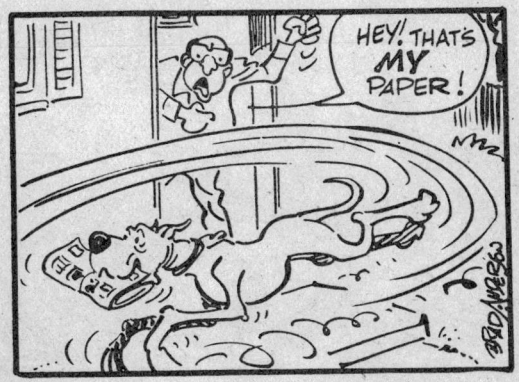

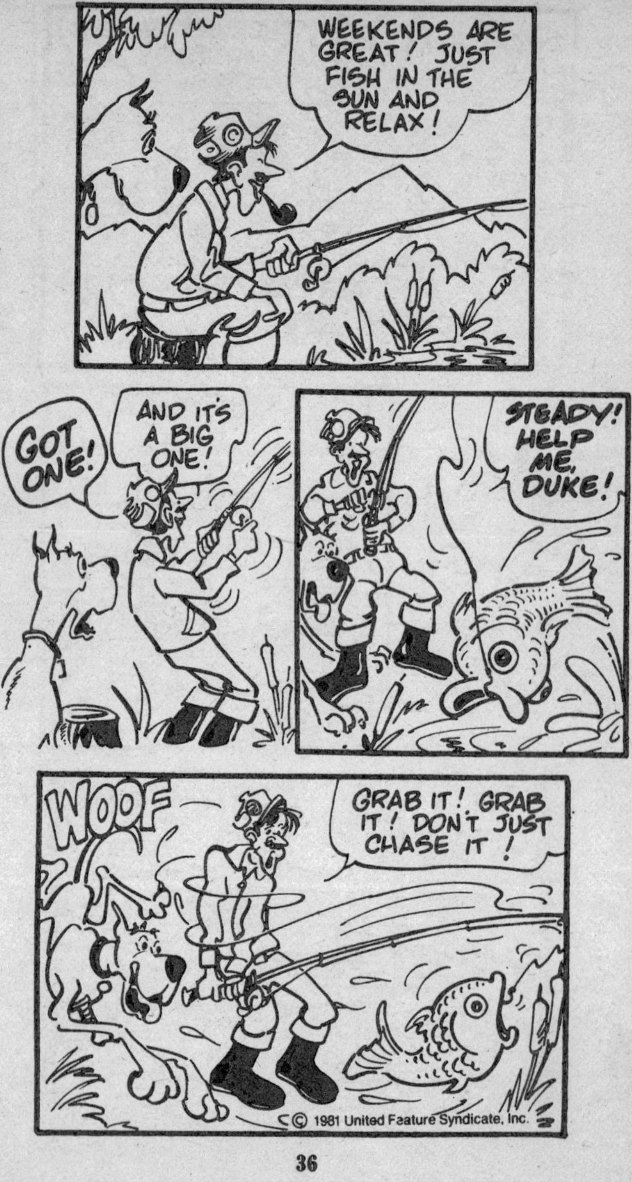
WEEKENDS ARE GREAT! JUST FISH IN THE SUN AND RELAX!
GOT ONE!
AND IT'S A BIG ONE!
STEADY! HELP ME, DUKE!
WOOF
GRAB IT! GRAB IT! DON'T JUST CHASE IT!
© 1981 United Feature Syndicate, Inc.

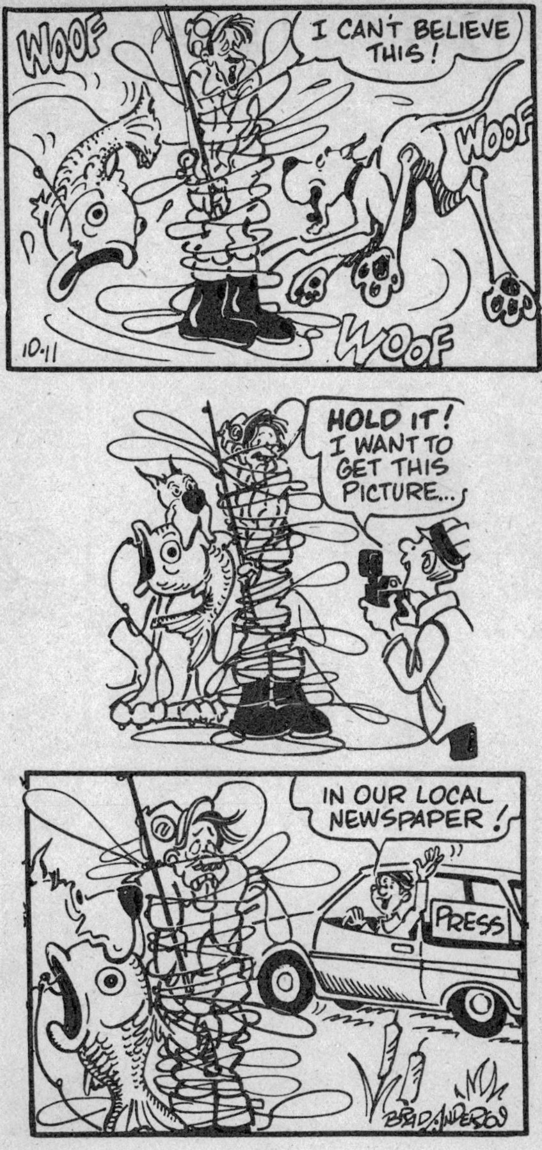
WOOF
I CAN'T BELIEVE THIS!
WOOF
WOOF
10.11
HOLD IT! I WANT TO GET THIS PICTURE...
IN OUR LOCAL NEWSPAPER!
PRESS
BRAD ANDERSON

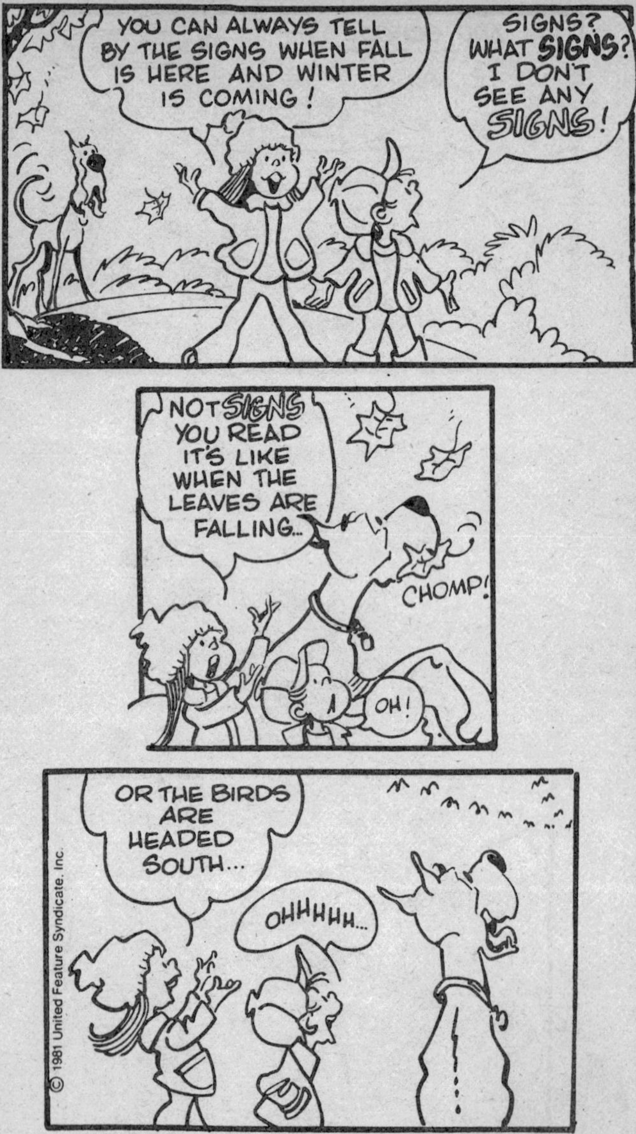
YOU CAN ALWAYS TELL BY THE SIGNS WHEN FALL IS HERE AND WINTER IS COMING!
SIGNS? WHAT SIGNS? I DON'T SEE ANY SIGNS!
NOT SIGNS YOU READ IT'S LIKE WHEN THE LEAVES ARE FALLING...
CHOMP!
OH!
OR THE BIRDS ARE HEADED SOUTH...
OHHHHH...

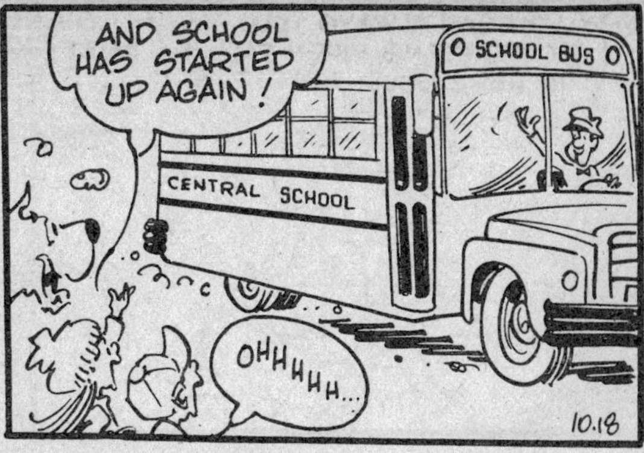
AND SCHOOL HAS STARTED UP AGAIN!
SCHOOL BUS
CENTRAL SCHOOL
OHHHHH...
10.18

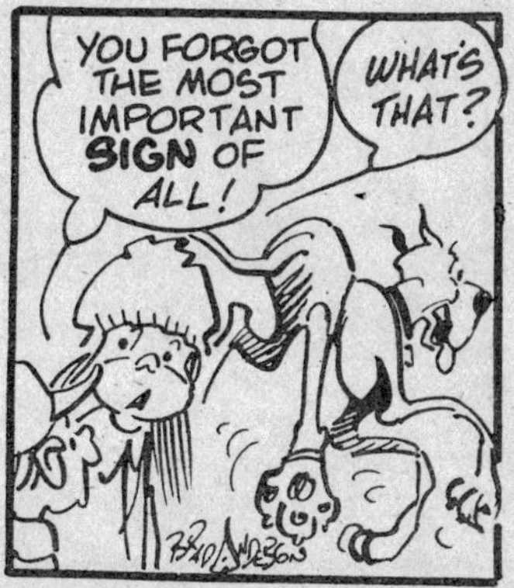
YOU FORGOT THE MOST IMPORTANT SIGN OF ALL!
WHAT'S THAT?

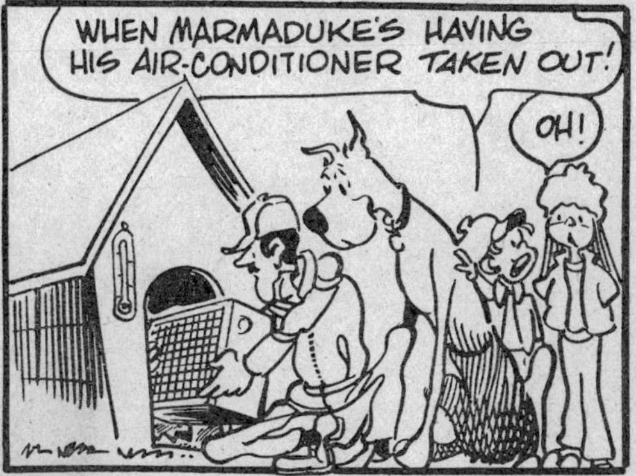
WHEN MARMADUKE'S HAVING HIS AIR-CONDITIONER TAKEN OUT!
OH!

CHIRP!
CHIRP! CHIRP!
WOOF! WOOF!

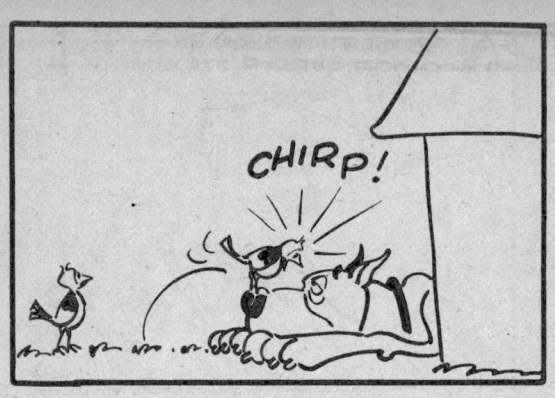

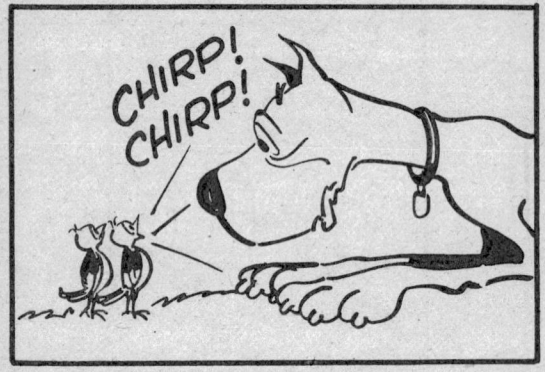

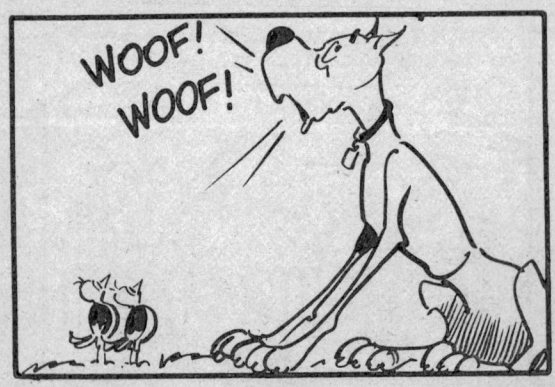

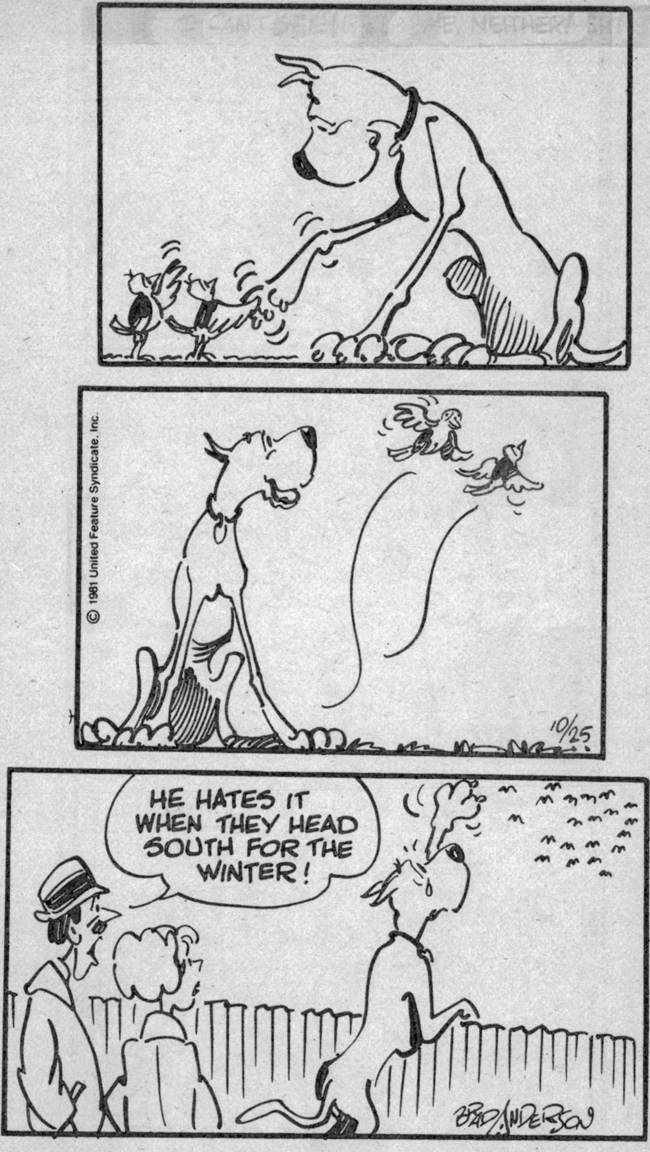
© 1981 United Feature Syndicate, Inc.
10/25
HE HATES IT WHEN THEY HEAD SOUTH FOR THE WINTER!
BRAD ANDERSON

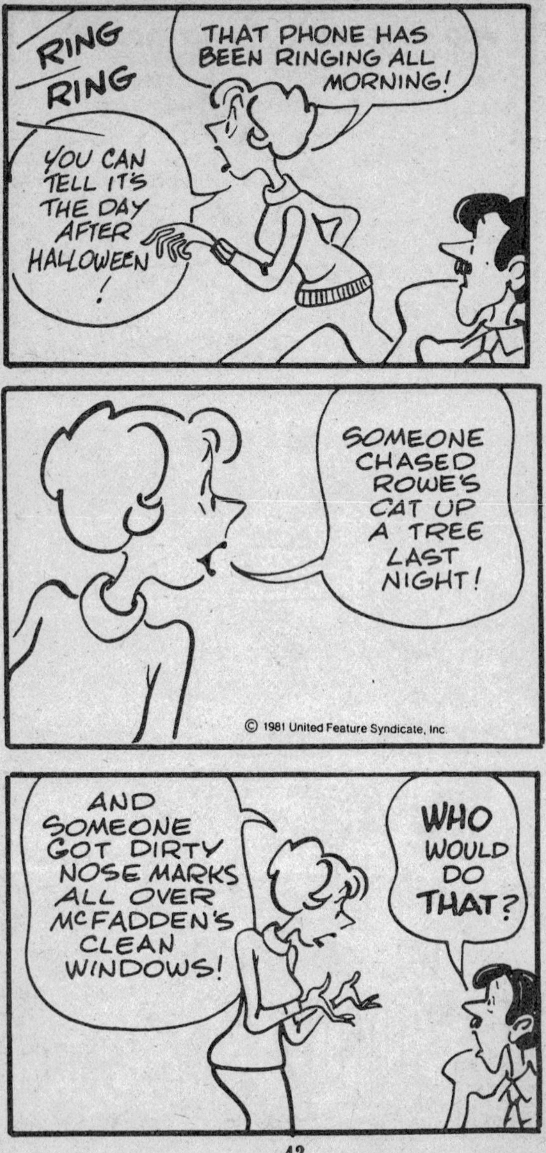
RING
RING
THAT PHONE HAS BEEN RINGING ALL MORNING!
YOU CAN TELL IT'S THE DAY AFTER HALLOWEEN!
SOMEONE CHASED ROWE'S CAT UP A TREE LAST NIGHT!
© 1981 United Feature Syndicate, Inc.
AND SOMEONE GOT DIRTY NOSE MARKS ALL OVER McFADDEN'S CLEAN WINDOWS!
WHO WOULD DO THAT?

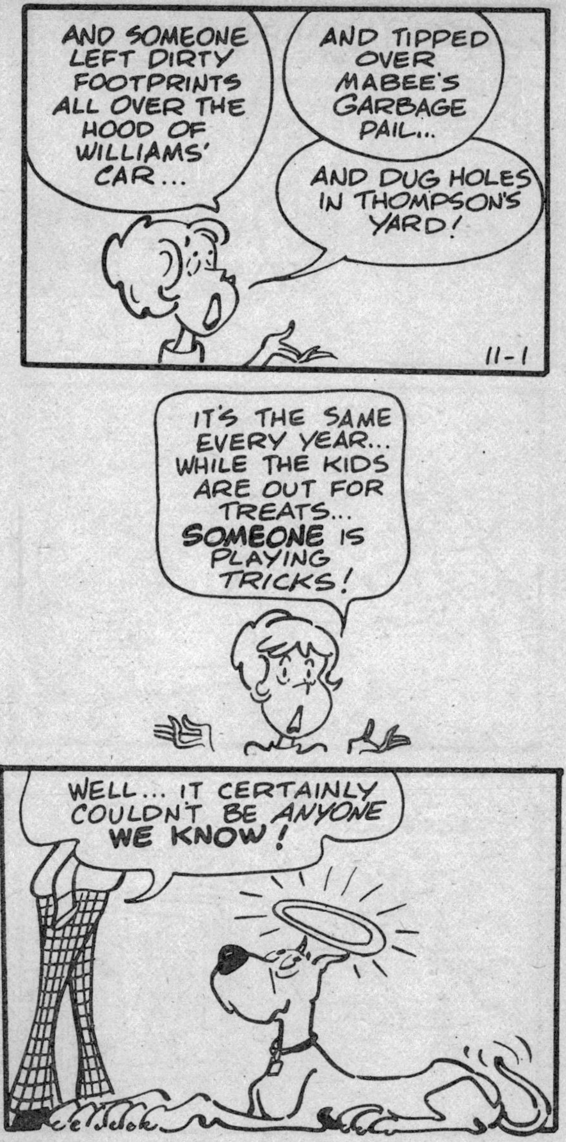
AND SOMEONE LEFT DIRTY FOOTPRINTS ALL OVER THE HOOD OF WILLIAMS' CAR...
AND TIPPED OVER MABEE'S GARBAGE PAIL...
AND DUG HOLES IN THOMPSON'S YARD!
11-1
IT'S THE SAME EVERY YEAR... WHILE THE KIDS ARE OUT FOR TREATS... SOMEONE IS PLAYING TRICKS!
WELL... IT CERTAINLY COULDN'T BE ANYONE WE KNOW!

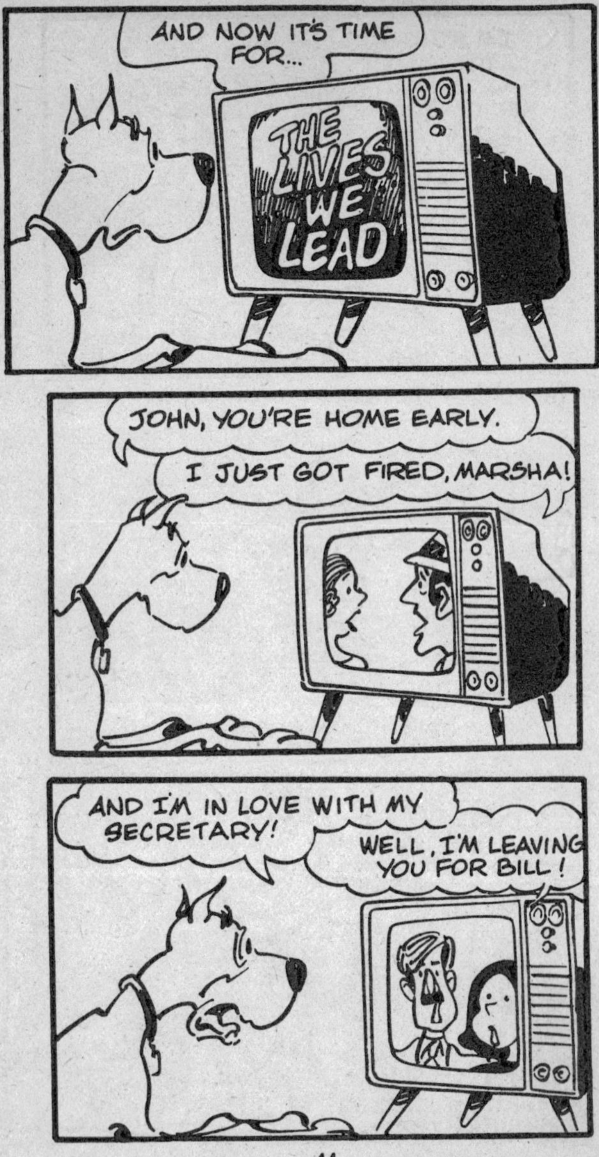
AND NOW IT'S TIME FOR...
THE LIVES WE LEAD
JOHN, YOU'RE HOME EARLY.
I JUST GOT FIRED, MARSHA!
AND I'M IN LOVE WITH MY SECRETARY!
WELL, I'M LEAVING YOU FOR BILL!

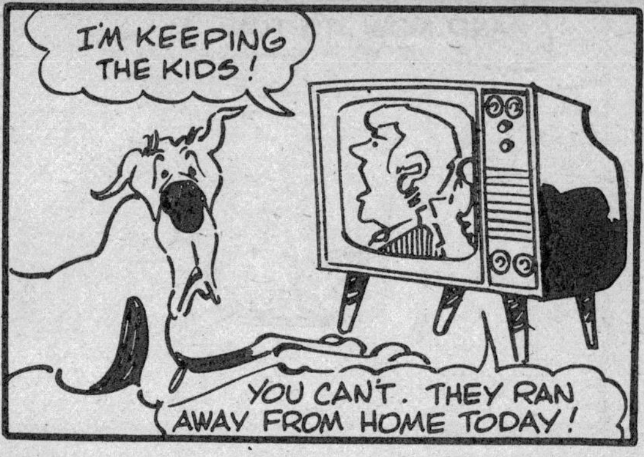
I'M KEEPING THE KIDS!
YOU CAN'T. THEY RAN AWAY FROM HOME TODAY!

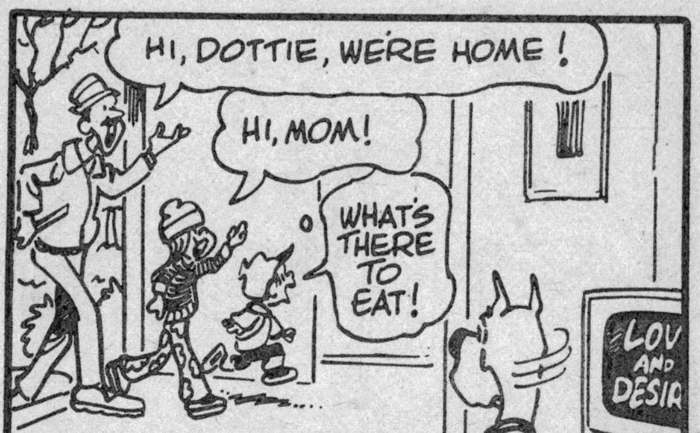
HI, DOTTIE, WE'RE HOME!
HI, MOM!
WHAT'S THERE TO EAT!
LOV AND DESIR
11-8

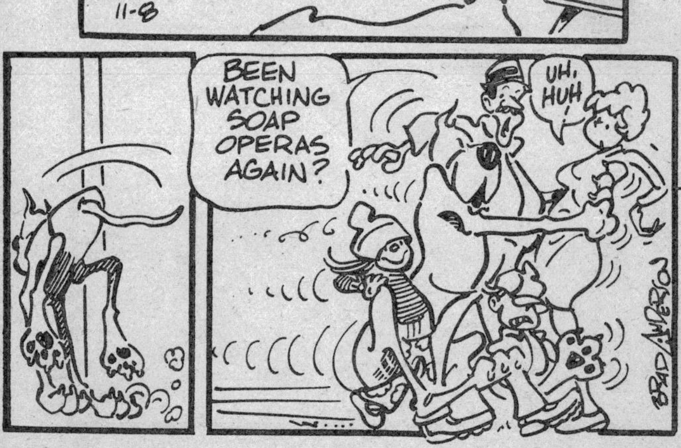
BEEN WATCHING SOAP OPERAS AGAIN?
UH, HUH!
BRAD ANDERSON

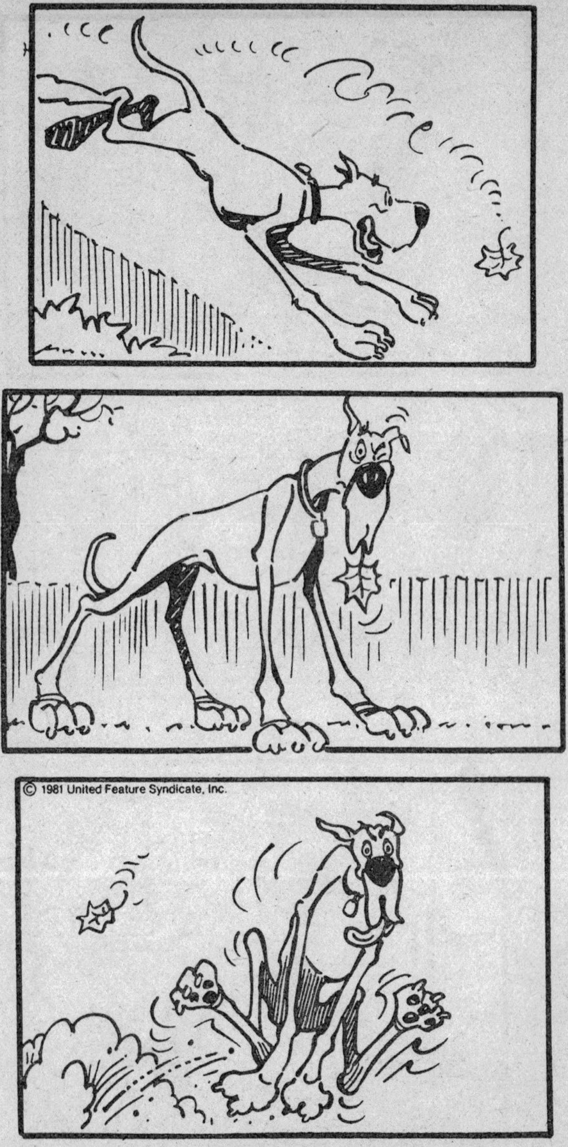
© 1981 United Feature Syndicate, Inc.

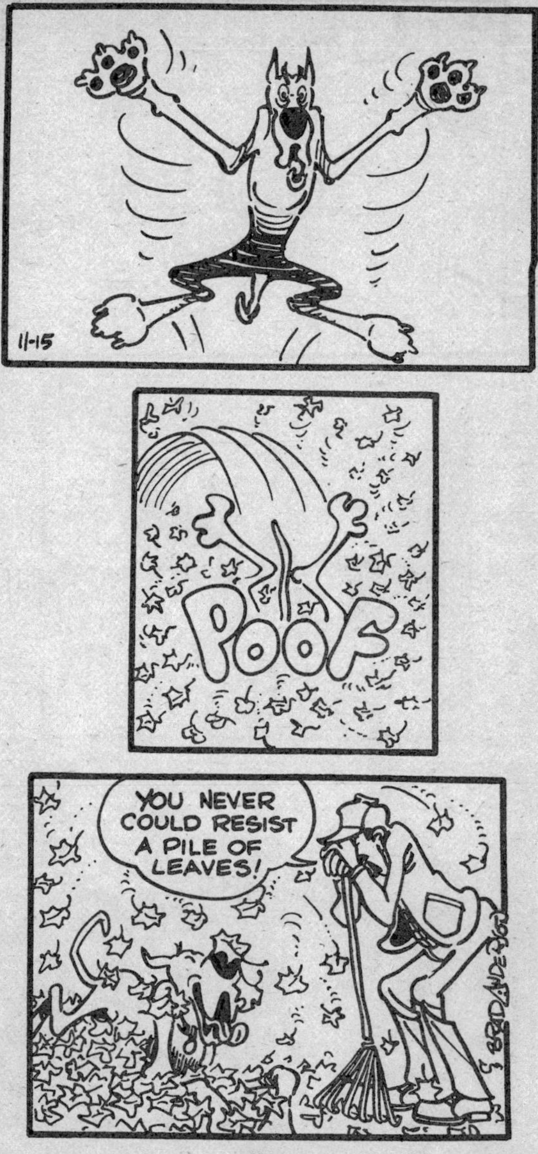
11-15
POOF
YOU NEVER COULD RESIST A PILE OF LEAVES!
BRAD ANDERSON

AARROOOOOOOOOOOOOOOOOOOOO
AARROOO
OH. DEAR!
I CAN'T TAKE IT ANYMORE!
ARR AOOFF
I'M GOING TO TEACH THAT DOG A LESSON!
AARROOO
LET'S GET HIM!
YEH! SEE HOW YOU LIKE IT!
AARROOOO

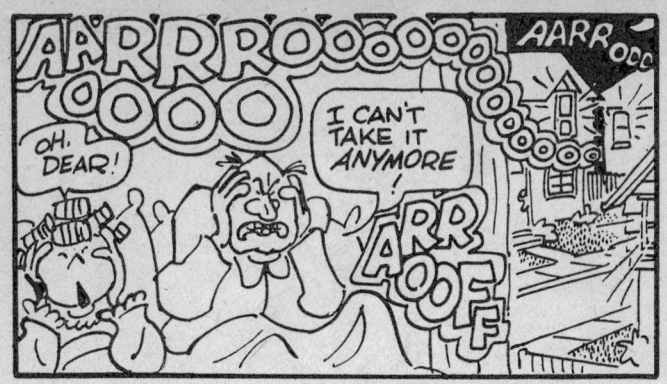

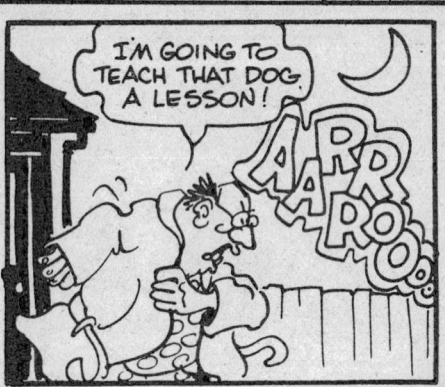

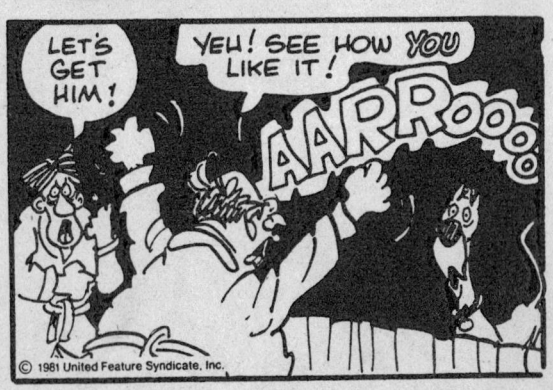

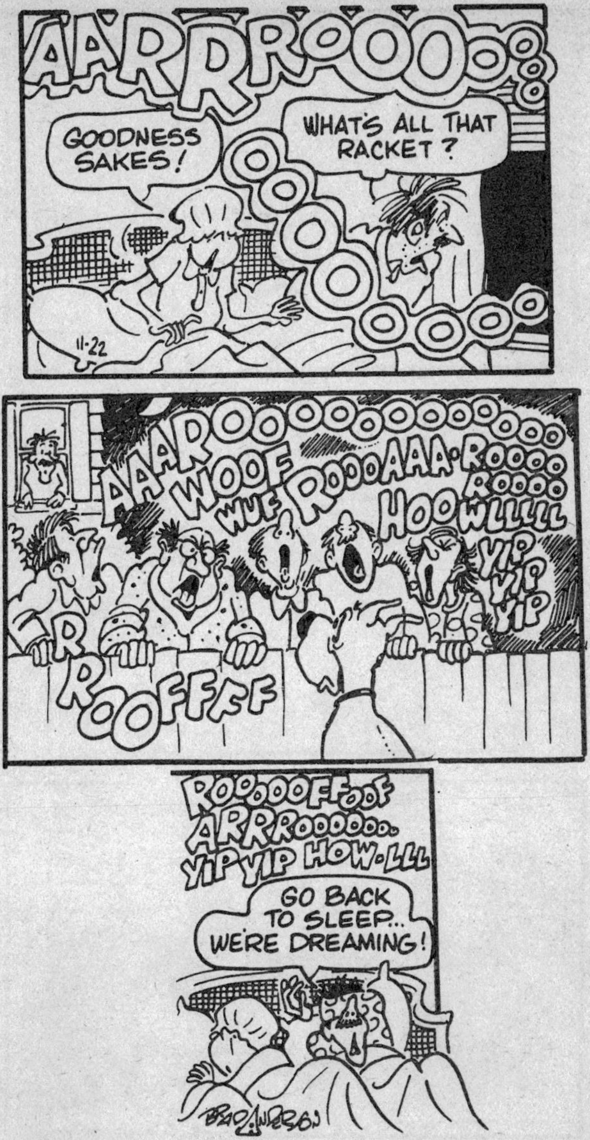

AARROOOOOOO
GOODNESS SAKES!
WHAT'S ALL THAT RACKET?
OOOOOOOOO
11-22
AAAROOOOOOOOOOOOOOO
WOOF
WUF
ROOOAAA-ROOOOO
ROOOOO
HOOWLLLLL
YIP YIP YIP
RROOFFFFF
ROOOOOOFFOOF
ARRROOOOOOO..
YIPYIP HOW-LLL
GO BACK TO SLEEP... WE'RE DREAMING!
BRAD ANDERSON

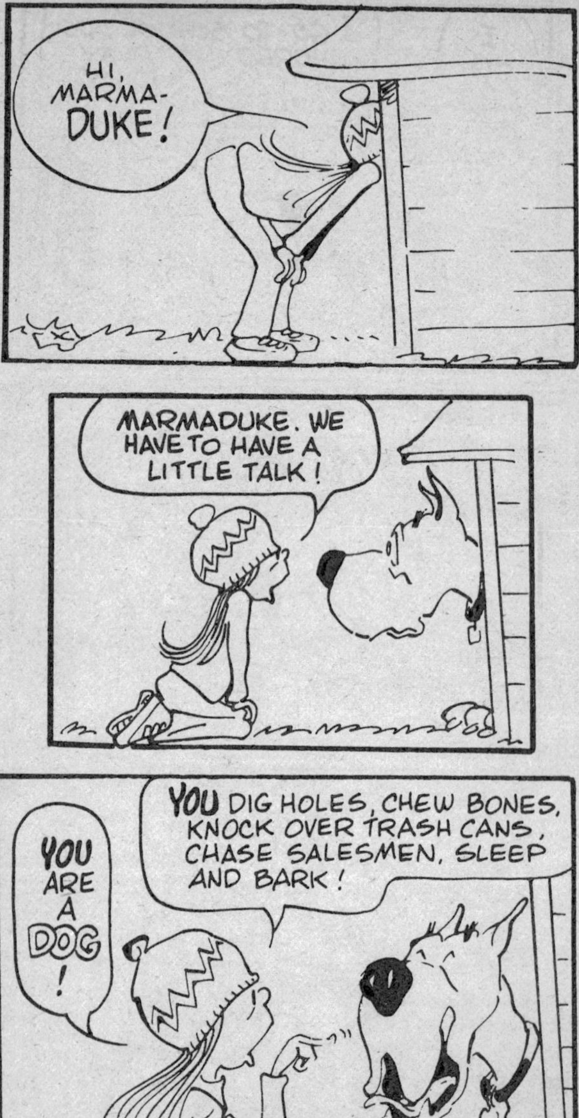
HI, MARMA-DUKE!
MARMADUKE. WE HAVE TO HAVE A LITTLE TALK!
YOU ARE A DOG!
YOU DIG HOLES, CHEW BONES, KNOCK OVER TRASH CANS, CHASE SALESMEN, SLEEP AND BARK!

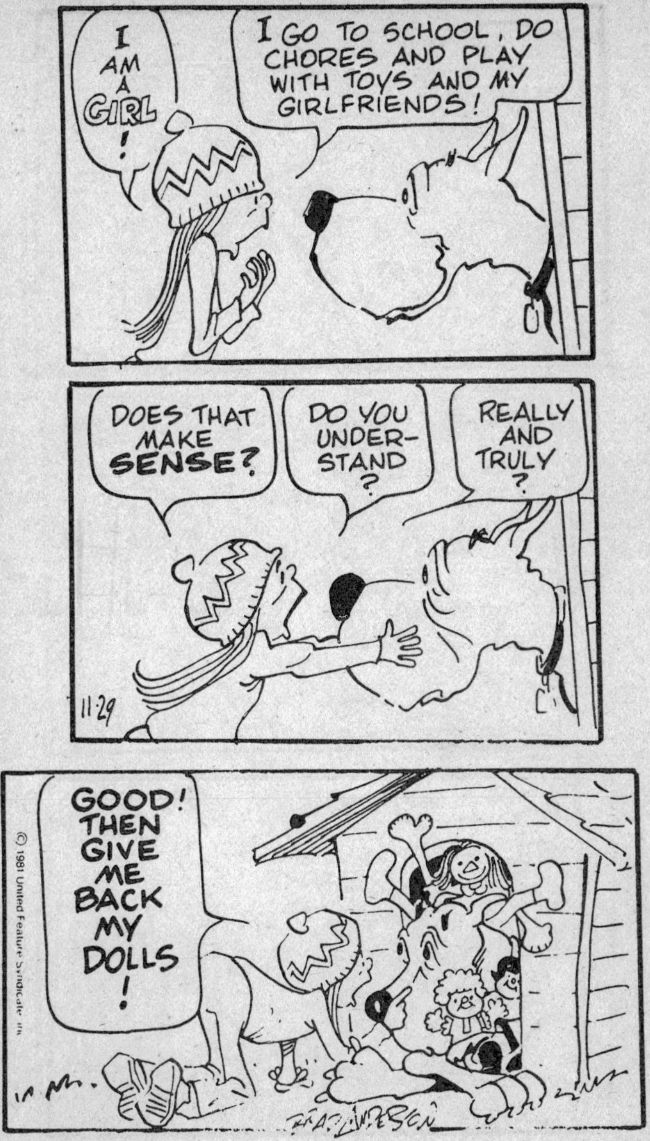
I AM A GIRL!
I GO TO SCHOOL, DO CHORES AND PLAY WITH TOYS AND MY GIRLFRIENDS!
DOES THAT MAKE SENSE?
DO YOU UNDER-STAND?
REALLY AND TRULY?
11-29
GOOD! THEN GIVE ME BACK MY DOLLS!
© 1981 United Feature Syndicate

MORE COFFEE ?
WHERE DOES THE TIME GO ? I'VE BEEN HERE ALL MORNING !
WHAT TIME IS IT ?
IT'S A QUARTER PAST TWELVE ALREADY !
OH, NO!
© 1981 United Feature Syndicate, Inc.

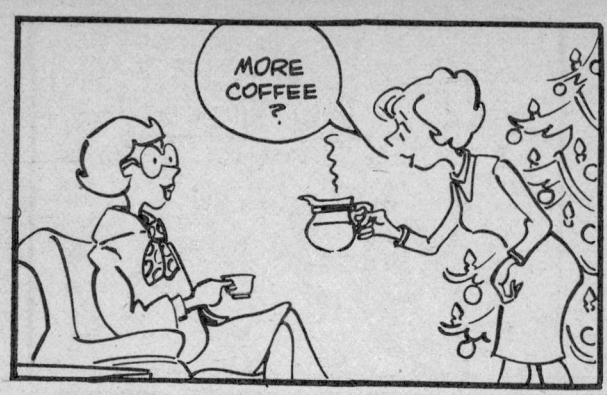

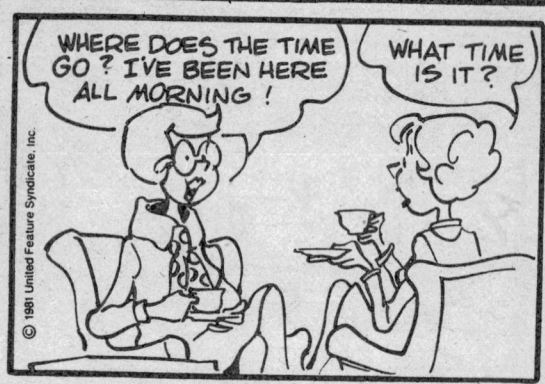

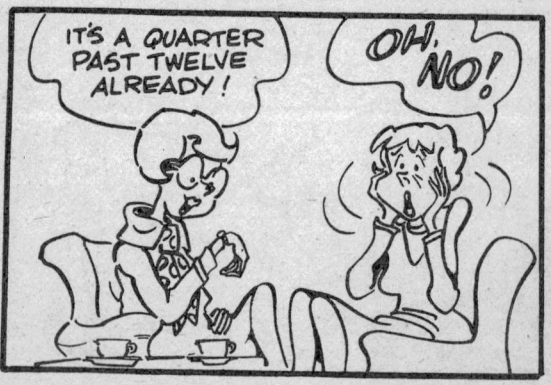

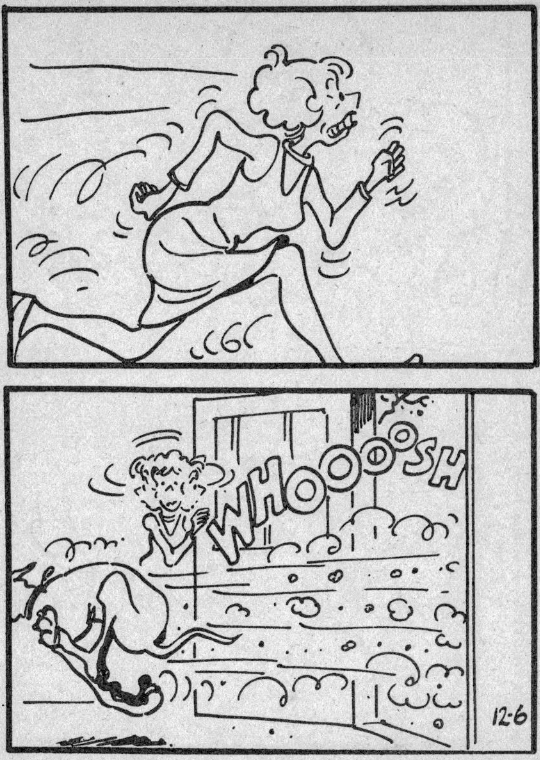
WHOOOOSH
12-6

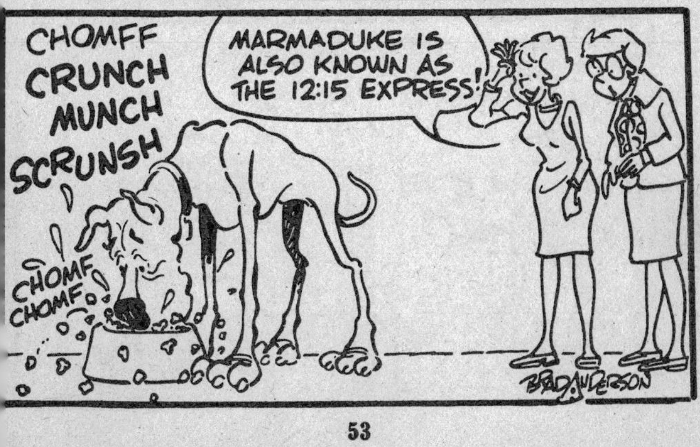
CHOMFF
CRUNCH
MUNCH
SCRUNSH
CHOMF
CHOMF
MARMADUKE IS ALSO KNOWN AS THE 12:15 EXPRESS!
BRAD ANDERSON

ARRRRMMMMM
MARMADUKE OFF THAT SOFA!
SLAP!
POOR, DUKE! HE FEELS SO UNLOVED!
I'LL FIX THAT!
I HAVE TO DO SOME CHRISTMAS SHOPPING.

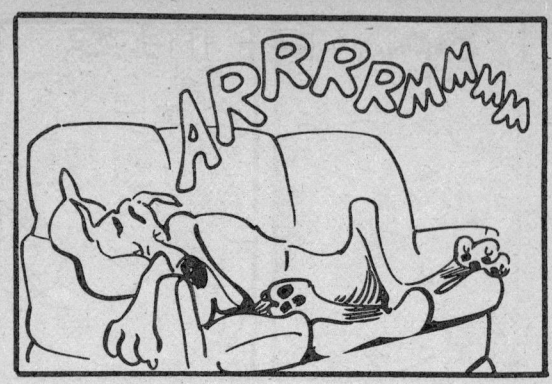

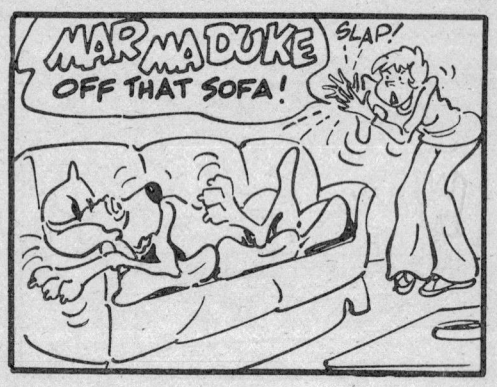

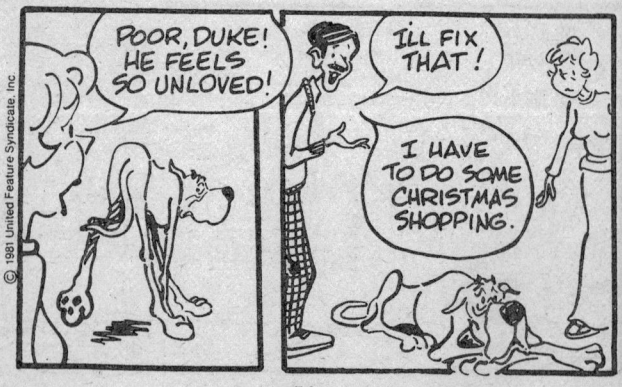

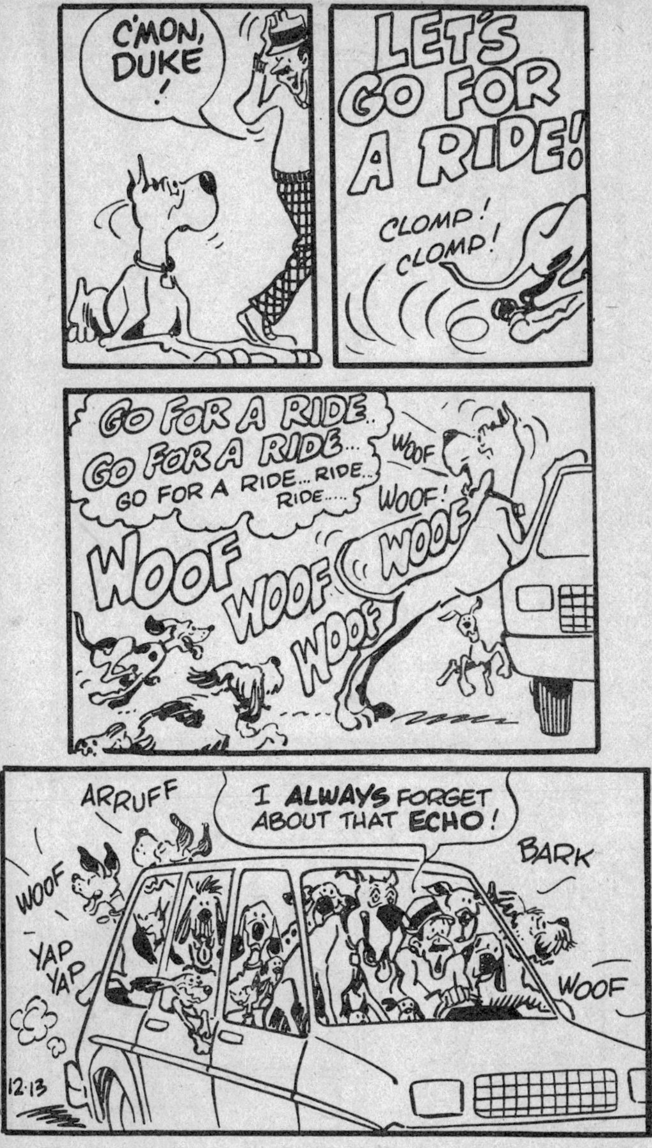

C'MON, DUKE !
LET'S GO FOR A RIDE!
CLOMP! CLOMP!
GO FOR A RIDE.. GO FOR A RIDE... GO FOR A RIDE... RIDE.. RIDE.....
WOOF
WOOF!
WOOF
WOOF
WOOF
WOOF
ARRUFF
I ALWAYS FORGET ABOUT THAT ECHO!
BARK
WOOF
YAP YAP
WOOF
12·13

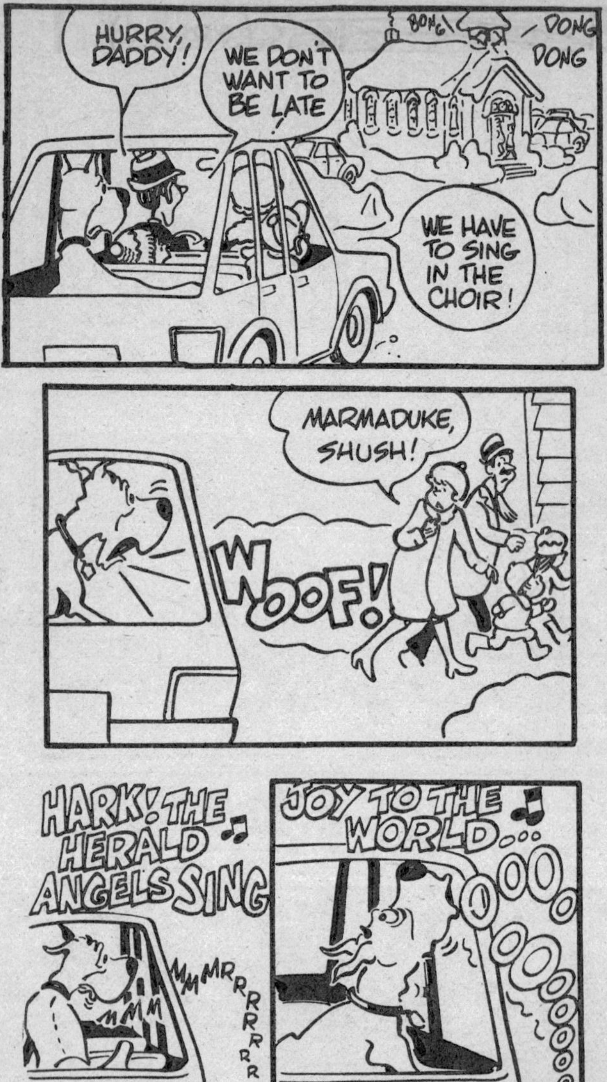
HURRY, DADDY!
WE DON'T WANT TO BE LATE
BONG
DONG DONG
WE HAVE TO SING IN THE CHOIR!
MARMADUKE, SHUSH!
WOOF!
HARK! THE HERALD ANGELS SING
MMMM
MMMRRRRRRR
JOY TO THE WORLD...
OOOOOOOOOOOOOOOO

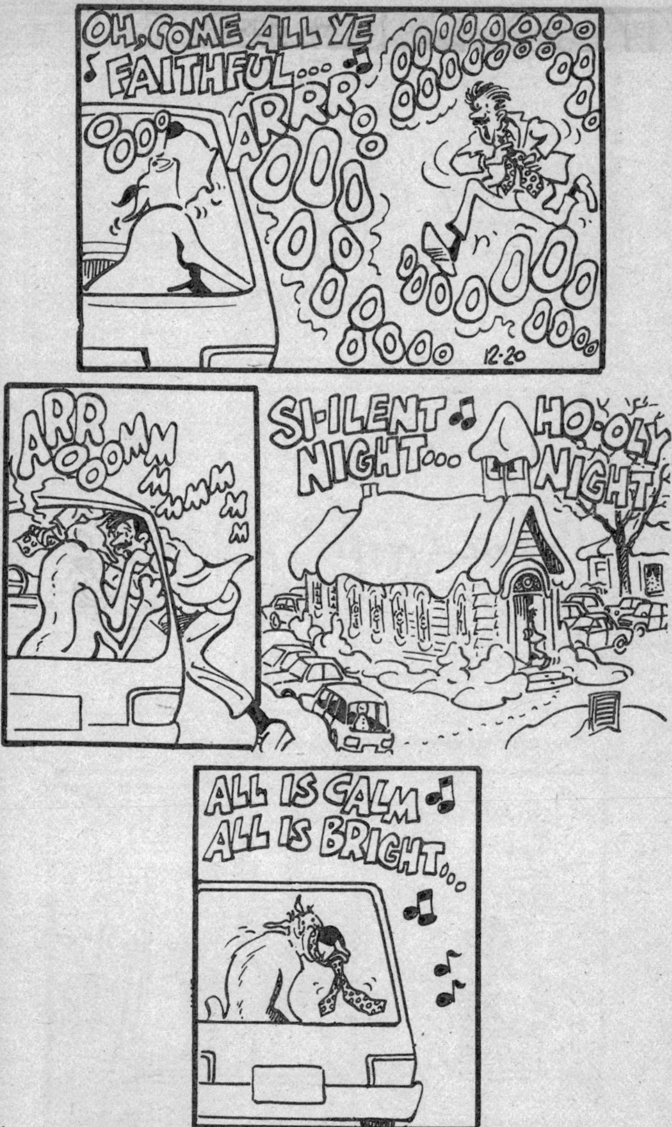

OH, COME ALL YE FAITHFUL...
ARRROOOO
12-20
ARROOOMMMMMMMM
SI-ILENT NIGHT...
HO-OLY NIGHT
ALL IS CALM
ALL IS BRIGHT...

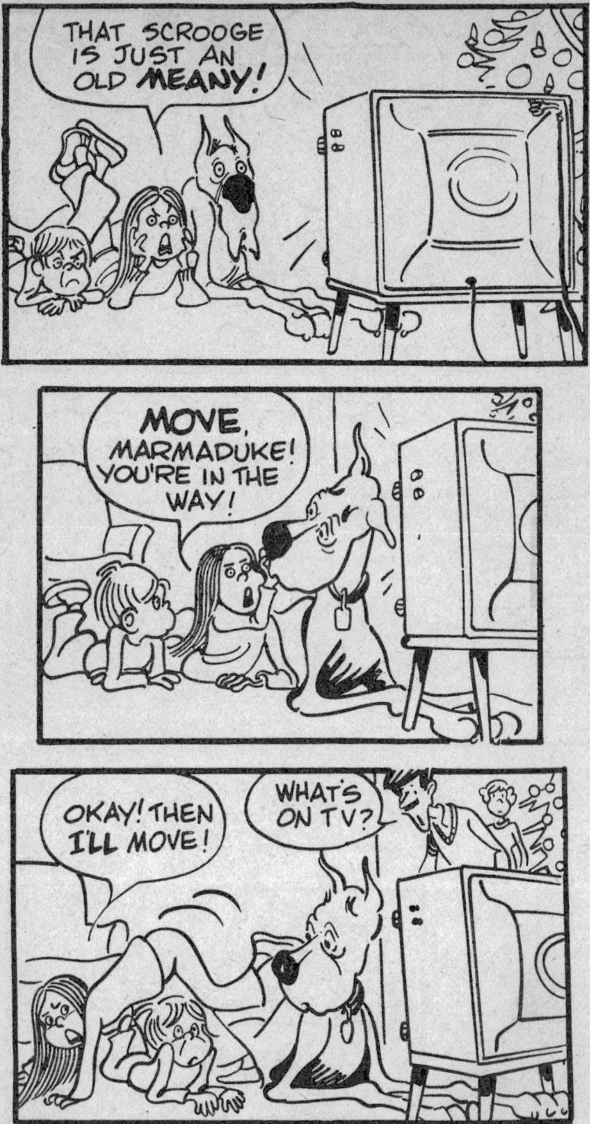
THAT SCROOGE IS JUST AN OLD MEANY!
MOVE, MARMADUKE! YOU'RE IN THE WAY!
OKAY! THEN I'LL MOVE!
WHAT'S ON TV?

"A CHRISTMAS CAROL" BY DICKENS.
THE GHOST OF CHRISTMAS FUTURE IS TALKING TO SCROOGE ... TINY TIM'S CHAIR IS EMPTY!
12·27
© 1981 United Feature Syndicate, Inc.
... AND MARMADUKE IS JUST WALLOWING IN SYMPATHY!

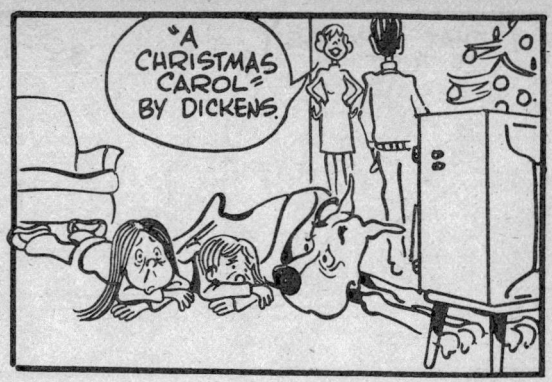

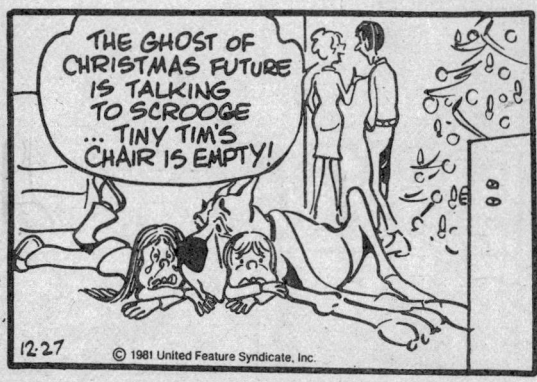

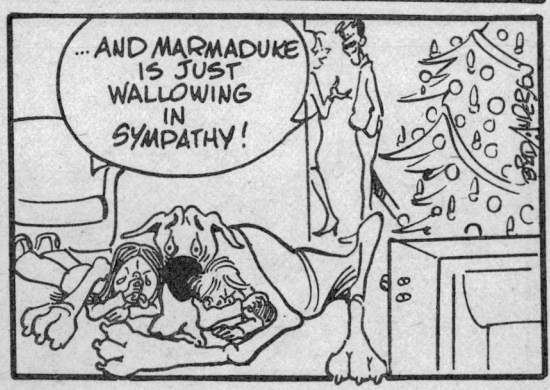

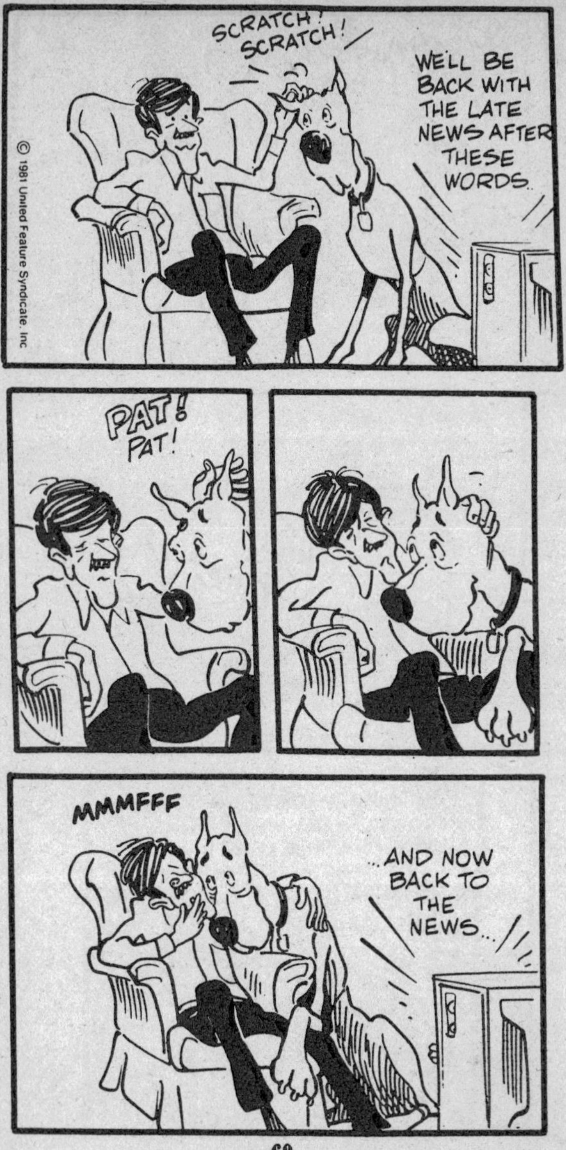
SCRATCH! SCRATCH!
WE'LL BE BACK WITH THE LATE NEWS AFTER THESE WORDS..
© 1981 United Feature Syndicate, Inc
PAT! PAT!
MMMFFF
...AND NOW BACK TO THE NEWS...

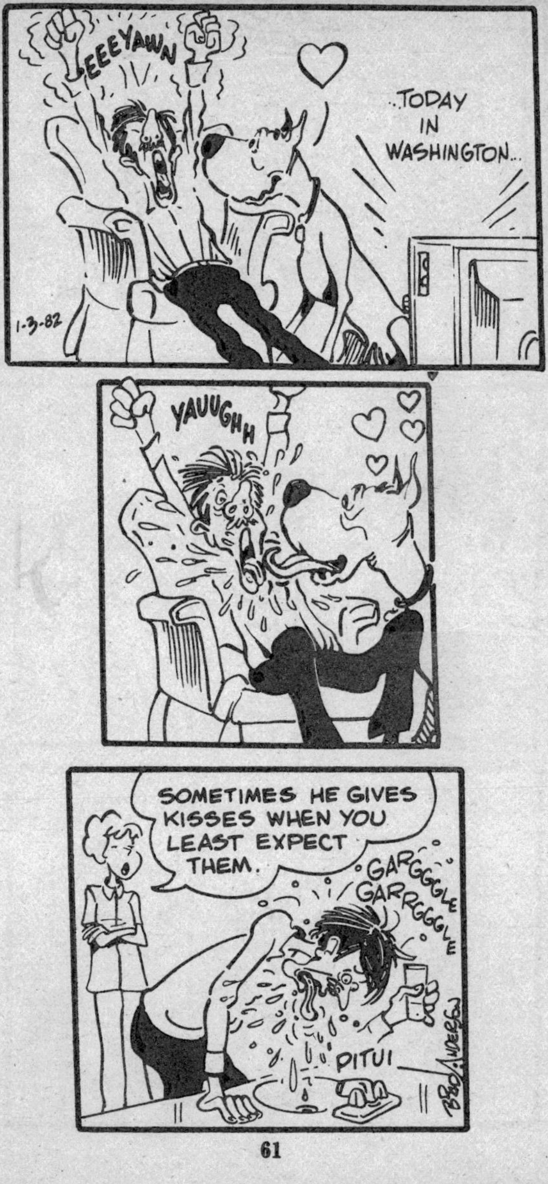
EEEEYAWN
...TODAY IN WASHINGTON...
1-3-82
YAUUGHH
SOMETIMES HE GIVES KISSES WHEN YOU LEAST EXPECT THEM.
GARGGGLE GARRGGGLE
PITUI
BRAD ANDERSON

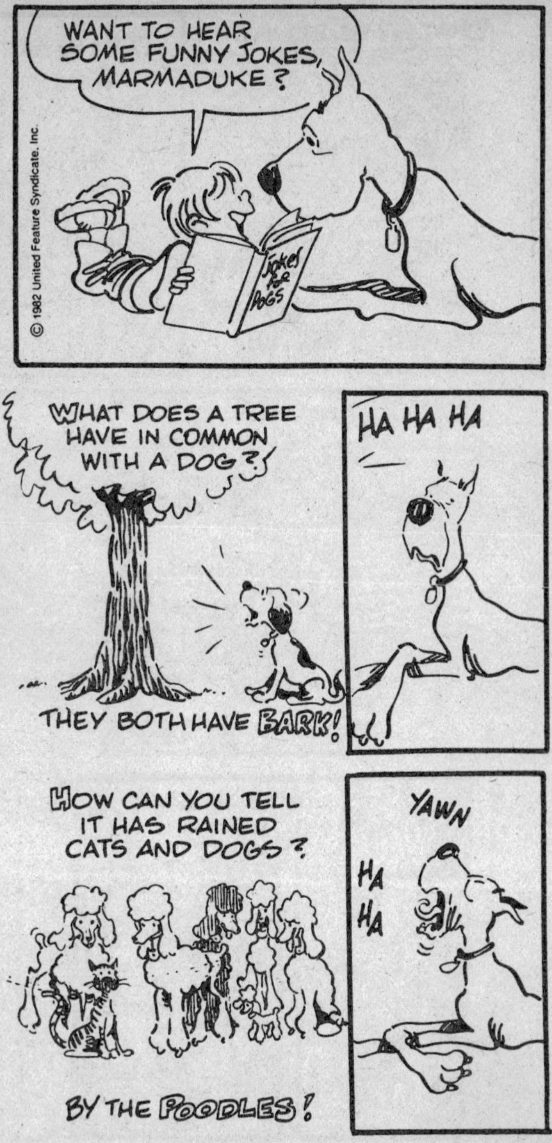
WANT TO HEAR SOME FUNNY JOKES, MARMADUKE?
JOKES FOR DOGS
© 1982 United Feature Syndicate, Inc.
WHAT DOES A TREE HAVE IN COMMON WITH A DOG?
THEY BOTH HAVE BARK!
HA HA HA
HOW CAN YOU TELL IT HAS RAINED CATS AND DOGS?
BY THE POODLES!
YAWN
HA HA

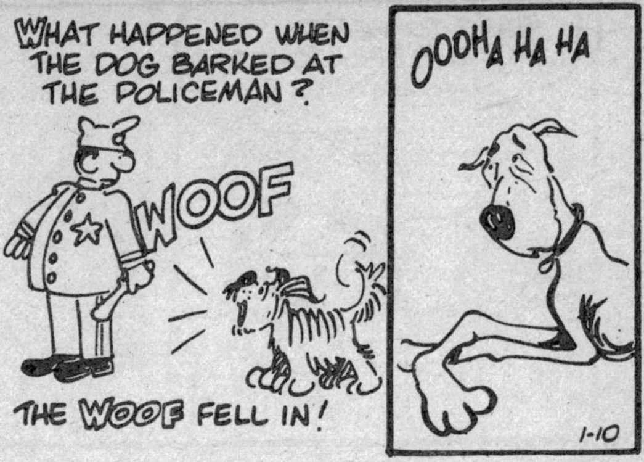
WHAT HAPPENED WHEN THE DOG BARKED AT THE POLICEMAN?
WOOF
THE WOOF FELL IN!
OOOH A HA HA
1-10

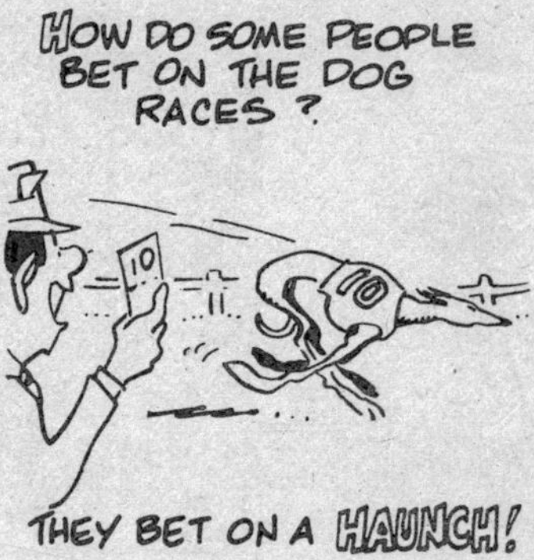
HOW DO SOME PEOPLE BET ON THE DOG RACES?
10
10
THEY BET ON A HAUNCH!

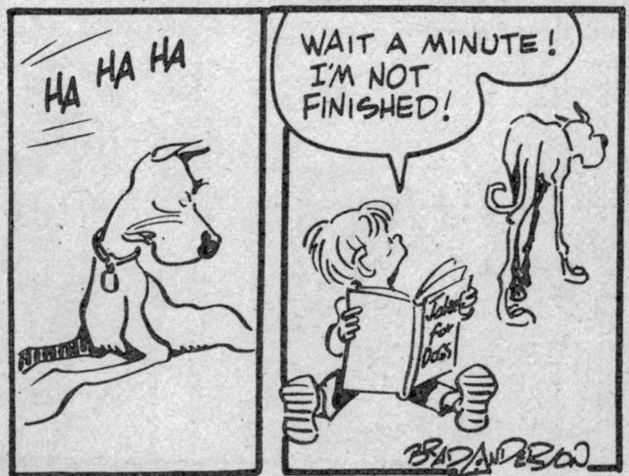
HA HA HA
WAIT A MINUTE! I'M NOT FINISHED!
Jokes for DOGS
BRAD ANDERSON

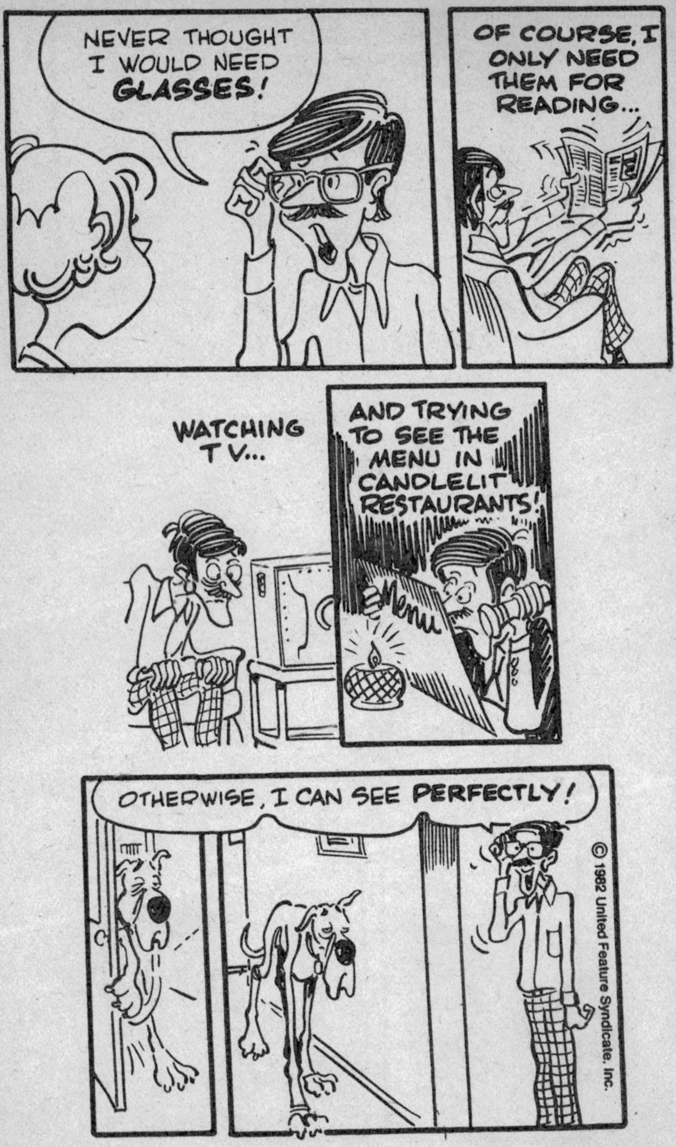
NEVER THOUGHT I WOULD NEED GLASSES!
OF COURSE, I ONLY NEED THEM FOR READING...
WATCHING T V...
AND TRYING TO SEE THE MENU IN CANDLELIT RESTAURANTS!
Menu
OTHERWISE, I CAN SEE PERFECTLY!
© 1982 United Feature Syndicate, Inc.

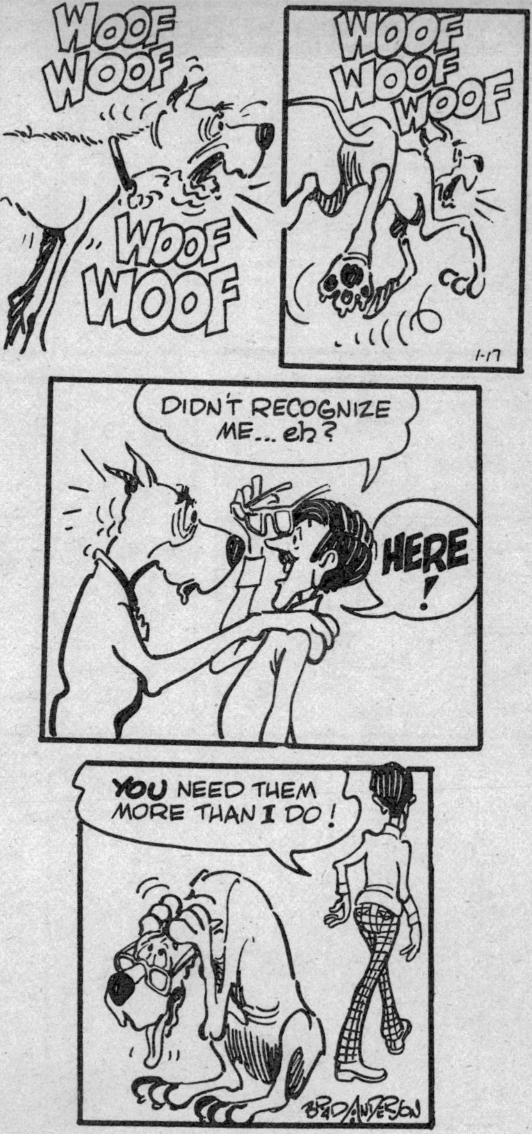
WOOF WOOF
WOOF WOOF
WOOF WOOF WOOF
1-17
DIDN'T RECOGNIZE ME... eh?
HERE!
YOU NEED THEM MORE THAN I DO!
BRAD ANDERSON

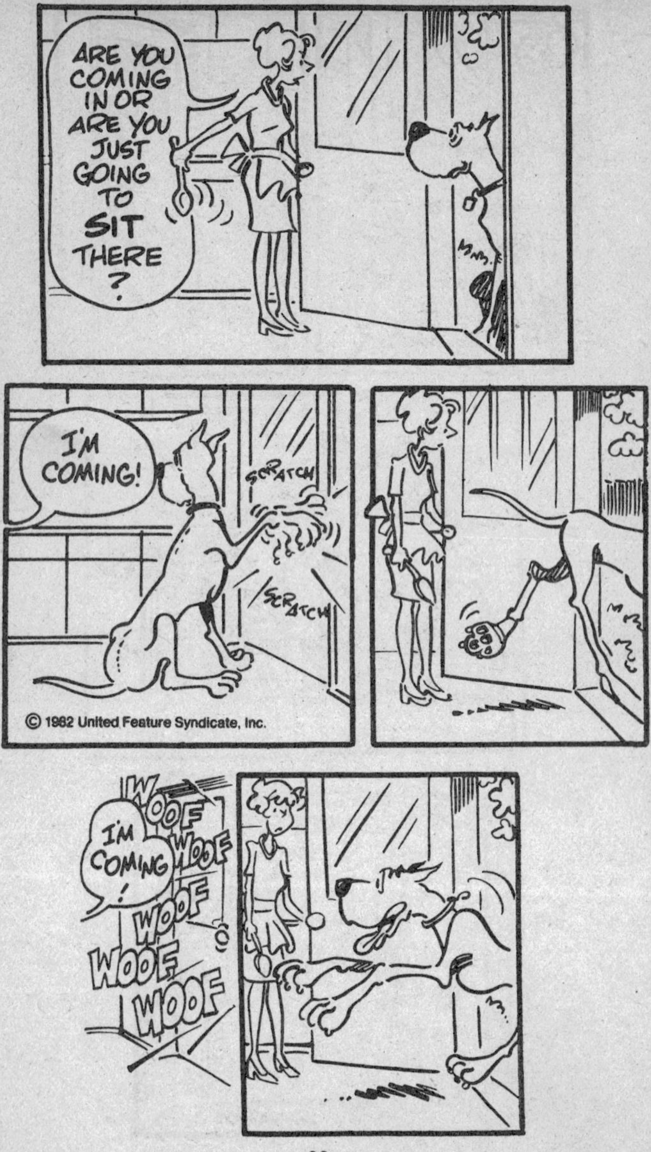
ARE YOU COMING IN OR ARE YOU JUST GOING TO SIT THERE?
I'M COMING!
SCRATCH
SCRATCH
I'M COMING!
WOOF
WOOF
WOOF
WOOF
WOOF
© 1982 United Feature Syndicate, Inc.

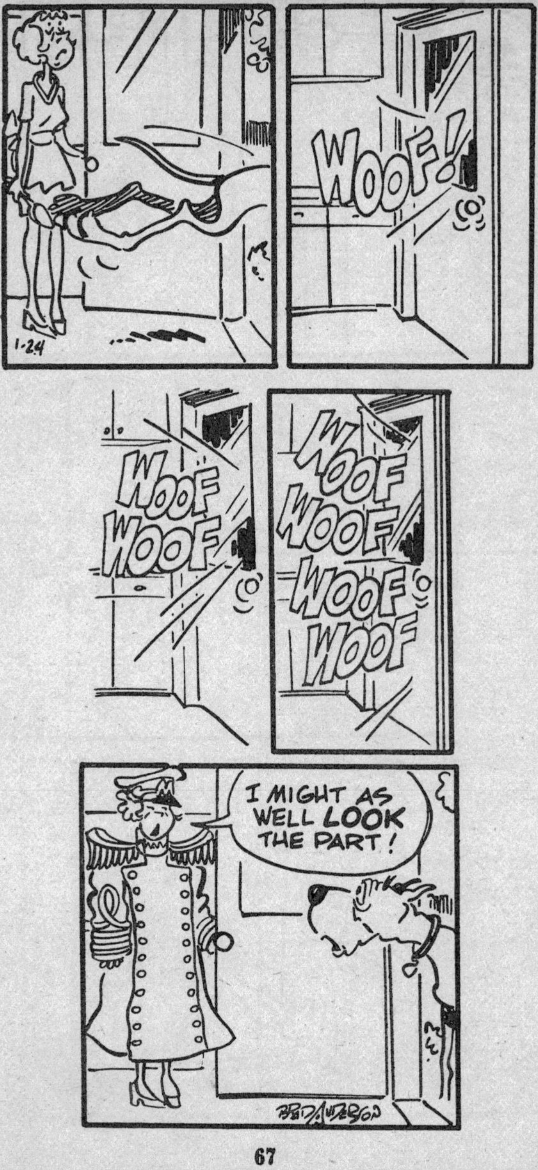
1·24
WOOF!
WOOF WOOF
WOOF WOOF WOOF WOOF
I MIGHT AS WELL LOOK THE PART!
BRAD ANDERSON

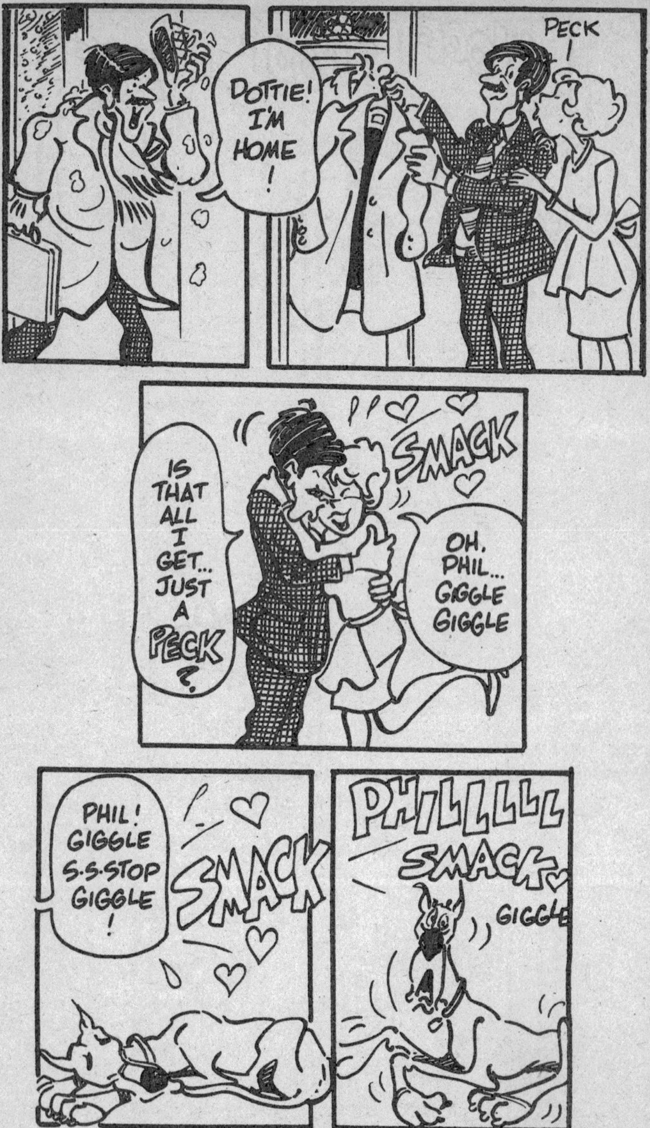

DOTTIE! I'M HOME !
PECK
IS THAT ALL I GET... JUST A PECK ?
SMACK
OH. PHIL... GIGGLE GIGGLE
PHIL! GIGGLE S-S-STOP GIGGLE !
SMACK
PHILLLLL
SMACK
GIGGLE

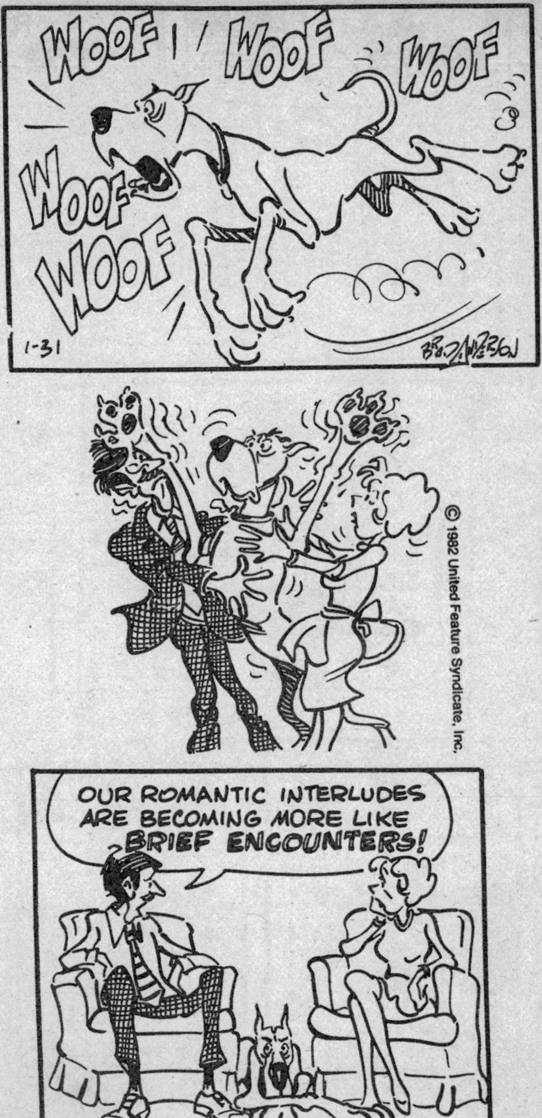
WOOF!! WOOF WOOF
WOOF
WOOF
1-31
OUR ROMANTIC INTERLUDES ARE BECOMING MORE LIKE BRIEF ENCOUNTERS!

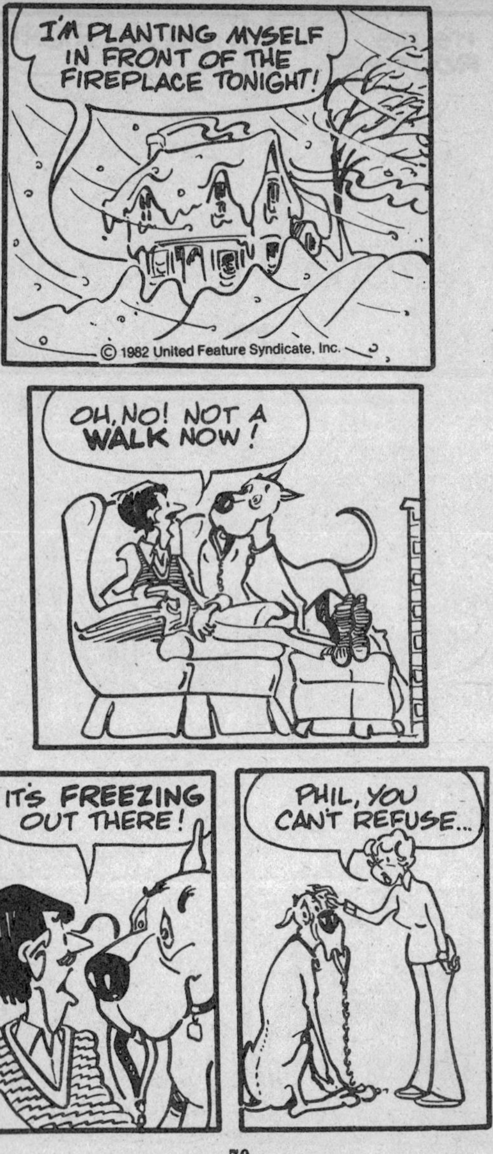
I'M PLANTING MYSELF IN FRONT OF THE FIREPLACE TONIGHT!
© 1982 United Feature Syndicate, Inc.
OH, NO! NOT A WALK NOW!
IT'S FREEZING OUT THERE!
PHIL, YOU CAN'T REFUSE...

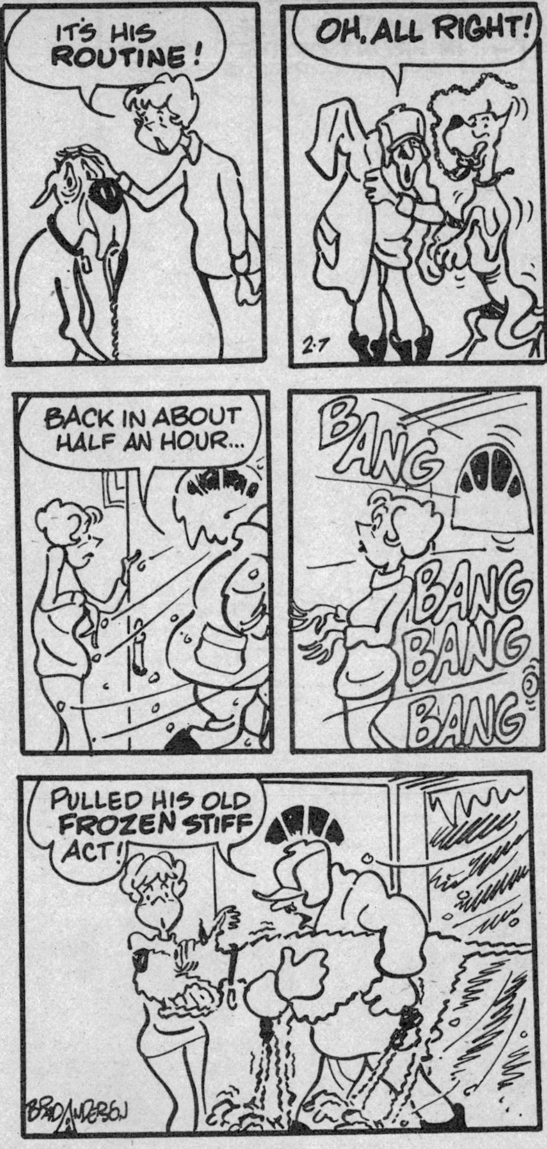
IT'S HIS ROUTINE!
OH, ALL RIGHT!
2-7
BACK IN ABOUT HALF AN HOUR...
BANG
BANG
BANG
BANG
PULLED HIS OLD FROZEN STIFF ACT!
BRAD ANDERSON

TODAY WE'LL READ SOME OF MARMADUKE'S LETTERS!
HE SURE GETS LOTS OF MAIL!

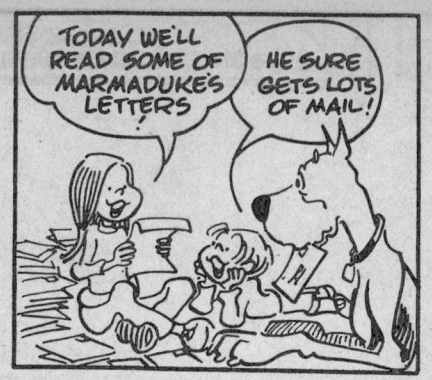

Here's one from Cherie Davis of Vancouver, Wa.

YIPES! THE PURSE BURGLAR STRIKES AGAIN!

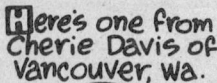

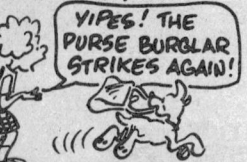

She says her dog DAISY gets in her mom's purse and snitches gum & candy.

Lee Johnson of Southlake, Tx. says his mama cat ran away and left her little kitten, so his grandmother's Eskimo dog named ADOLF adopted it. They eat together, play together and sleep together!

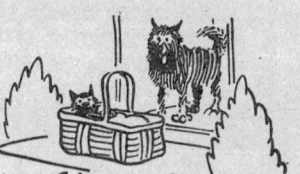

Brian Johnson of St. Louis, Mo. says his Lhasa apso, Lady Amanda, is very vain ...

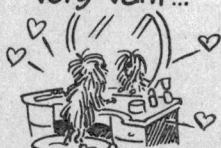

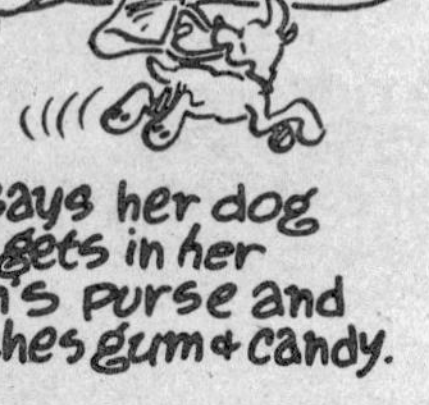

She jumps on the vanity bench to look at herself in the mirror!

And Mrs. Don Knowles of Federal Way, Va. says her miniature schnauzer has a very strange appetite ...

YOUR TONGUE IS...
GREEN!

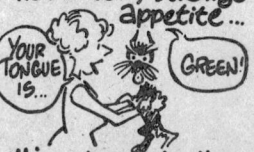

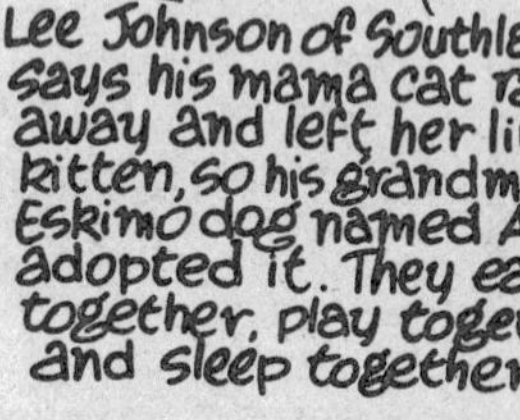

Missy inspects the strawberry bed and eats every plump GREEN strawberry

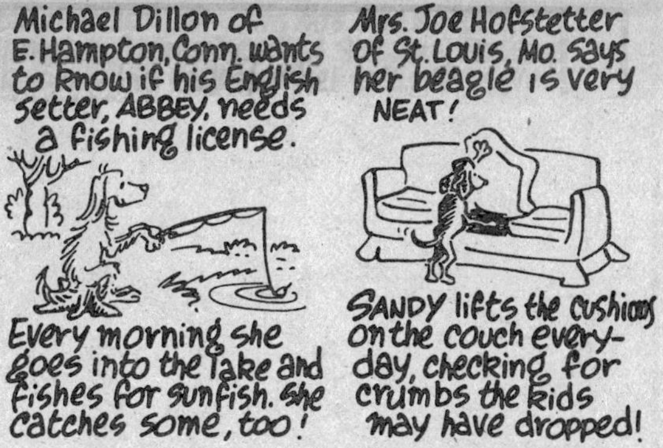
Michael Dillon of E. Hampton, Conn. wants to know if his English setter, ABBEY, needs a fishing license.
Every morning she goes into the lake and fishes for sunfish. She catches some, too!
Mrs. Joe Hofstetter of St. Louis, Mo. says her beagle is very NEAT!
SANDY lifts the cushions on the couch everyday, checking for crumbs the kids may have dropped!

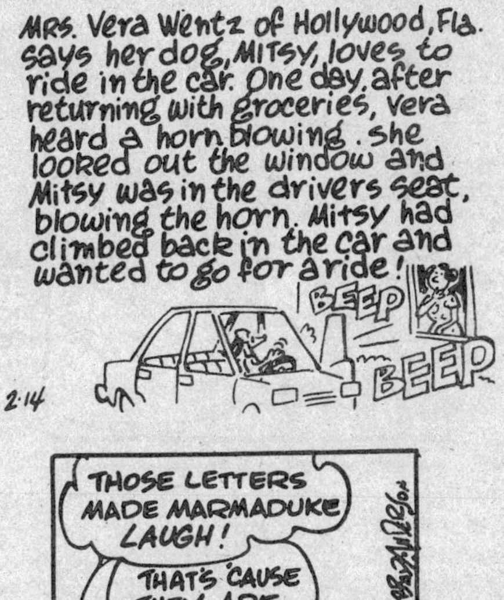
MRS. Vera Wentz of Hollywood, Fla. says her dog, MITSY, loves to ride in the car. One day, after returning with groceries, Vera heard a horn blowing. She looked out the window and Mitsy was in the drivers seat, blowing the horn. Mitsy had climbed back in the car and wanted to go for a ride!
BEEP
BEEP
2·14

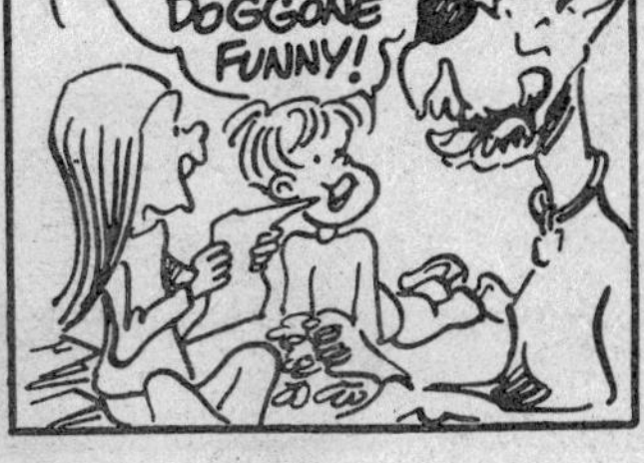
THOSE LETTERS MADE MARMADUKE LAUGH!
THAT'S 'CAUSE THEY ARE DOGGONE FUNNY!

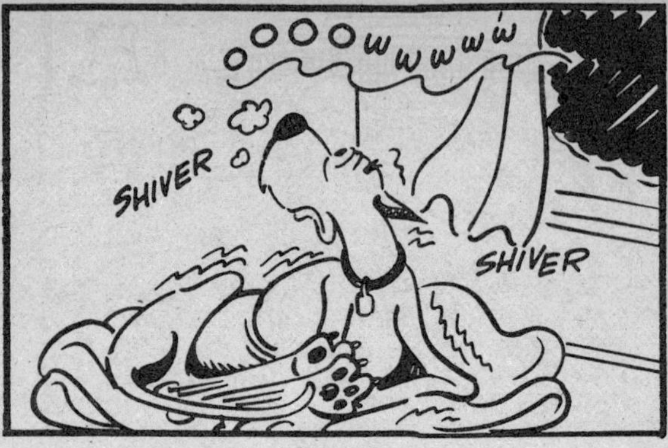
OOOOWWWWWW
SHIVER
SHIVER

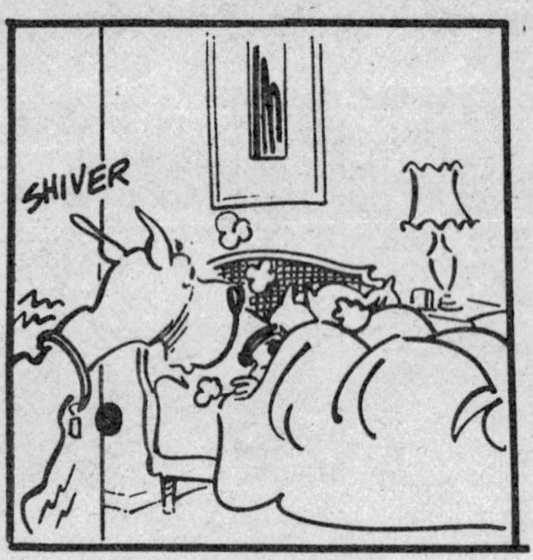
SHIVER

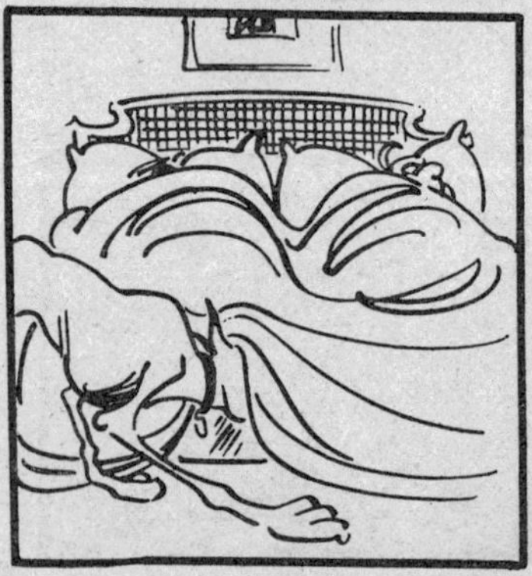

© 1982 United Feature Syndicate, Inc.
HE SURE KNOWS HOW TO HIJACK A WARM BED!
BRAD ANDERSON

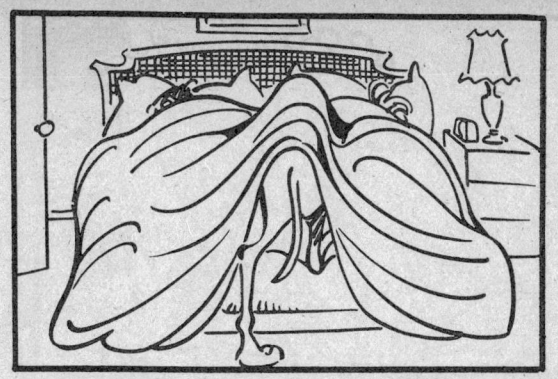

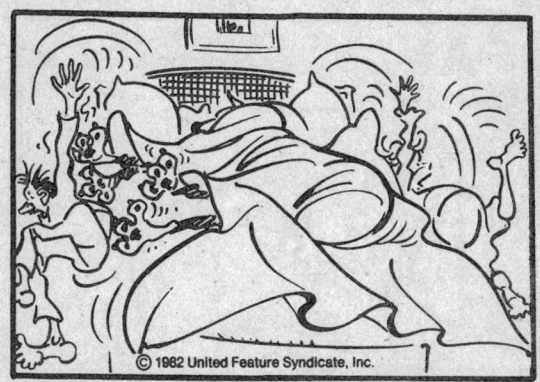

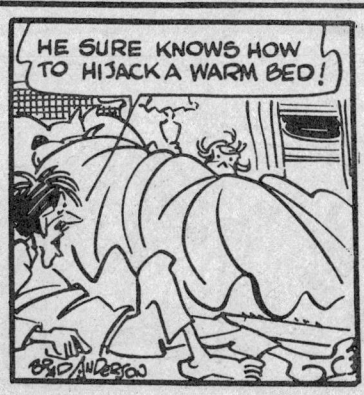

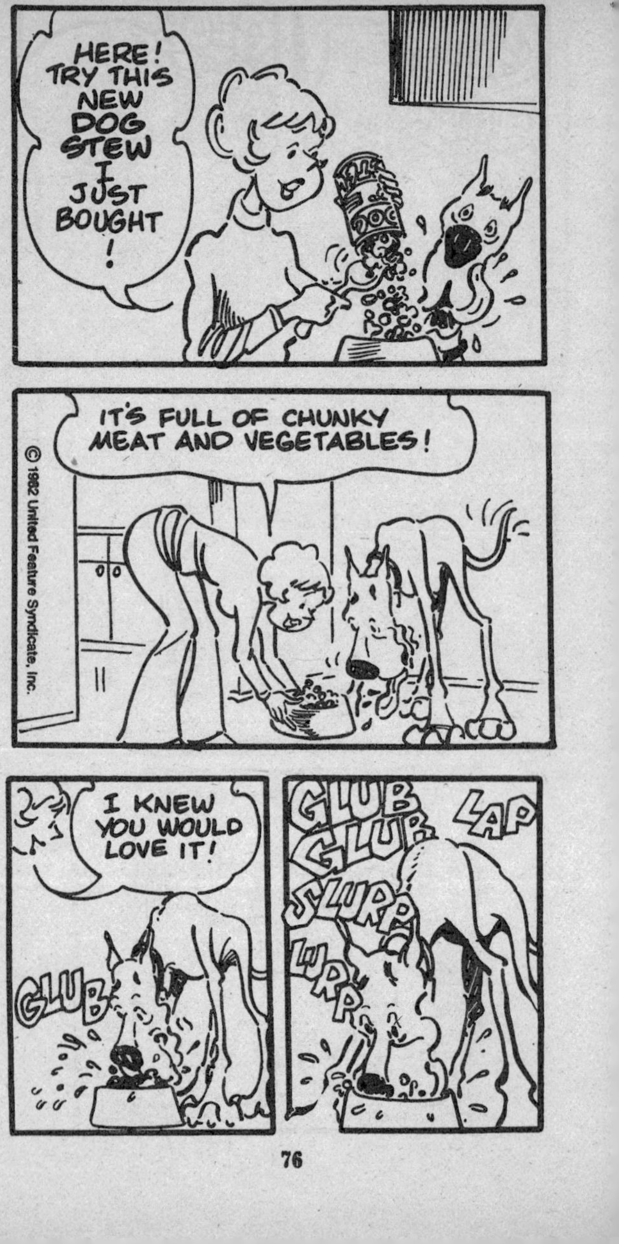
HERE! TRY THIS NEW DOG STEW I JUST BOUGHT!
IT'S FULL OF CHUNKY MEAT AND VEGETABLES!
I KNEW YOU WOULD LOVE IT!
GLUB
GLUB
GLUB
LAP
SLURP
LURP

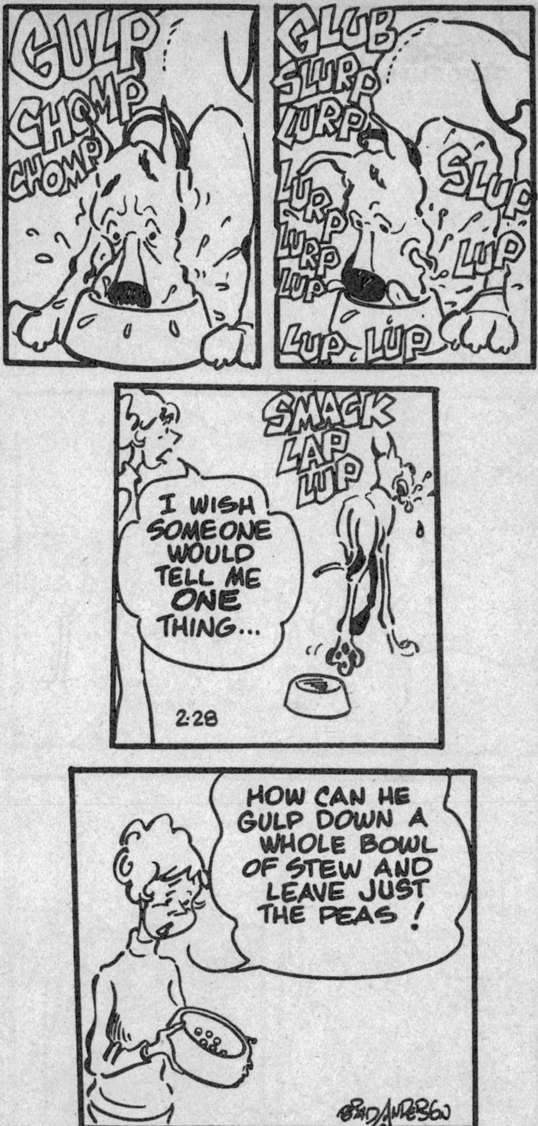
GULP
CHOMP
CHOMP
GLUB
SLURP
LURP
SLUP
LURP
LURP
LUP
LUP
LUP
LUP
SMACK
LAP
LUP
I WISH SOMEONE WOULD TELL ME ONE THING...
2·28
HOW CAN HE GULP DOWN A WHOLE BOWL OF STEW AND LEAVE JUST THE PEAS!
BRAD ANDERSON

FRESH
MEAT

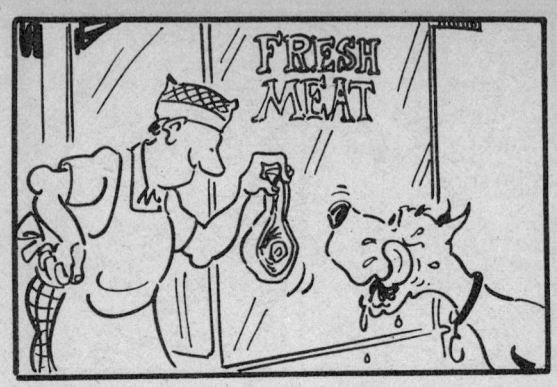

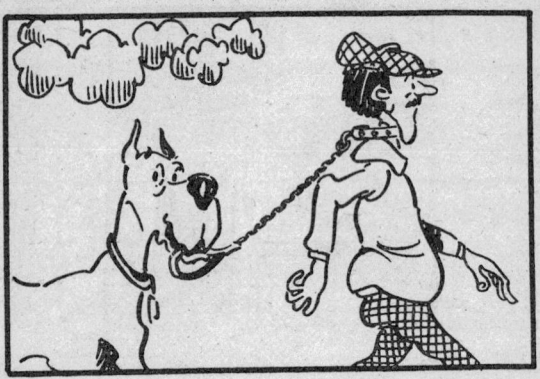

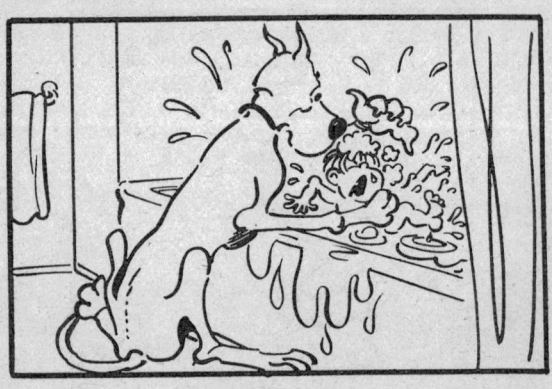

© 1982 United Feature Syndicate, Inc.
3·7
EVER NOTICE HOW SOMETIMES IT SEEMS HE'S SMILING WHEN HE SLEEPS?!
BRAD ANDERSON

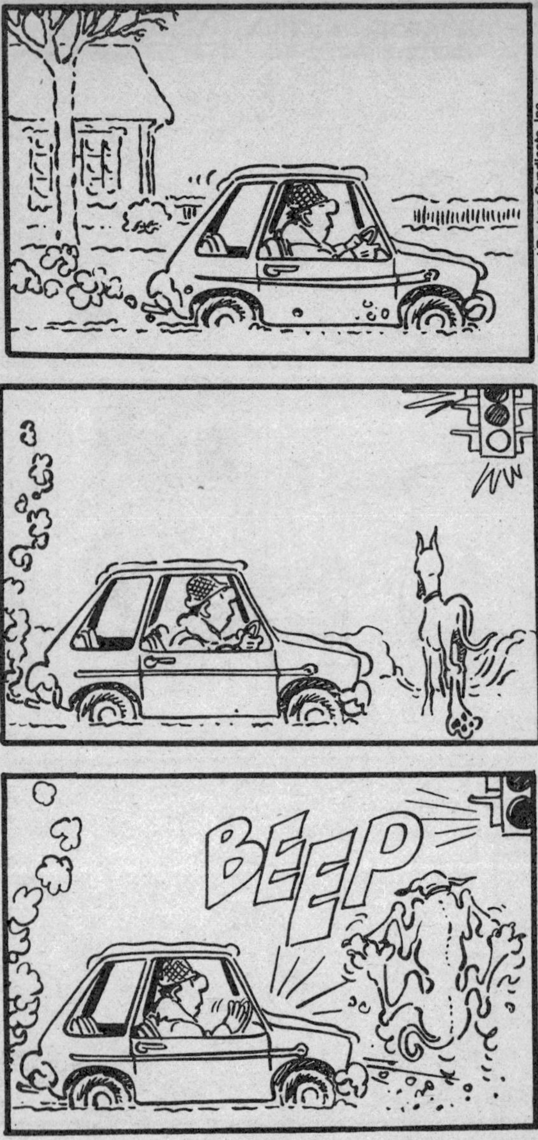
BEEP

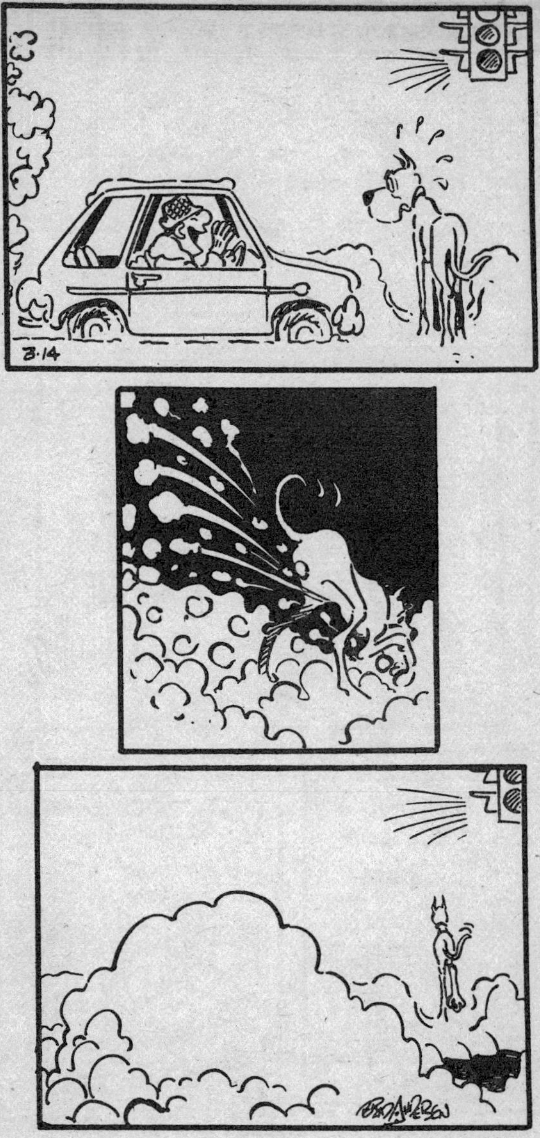
3.14

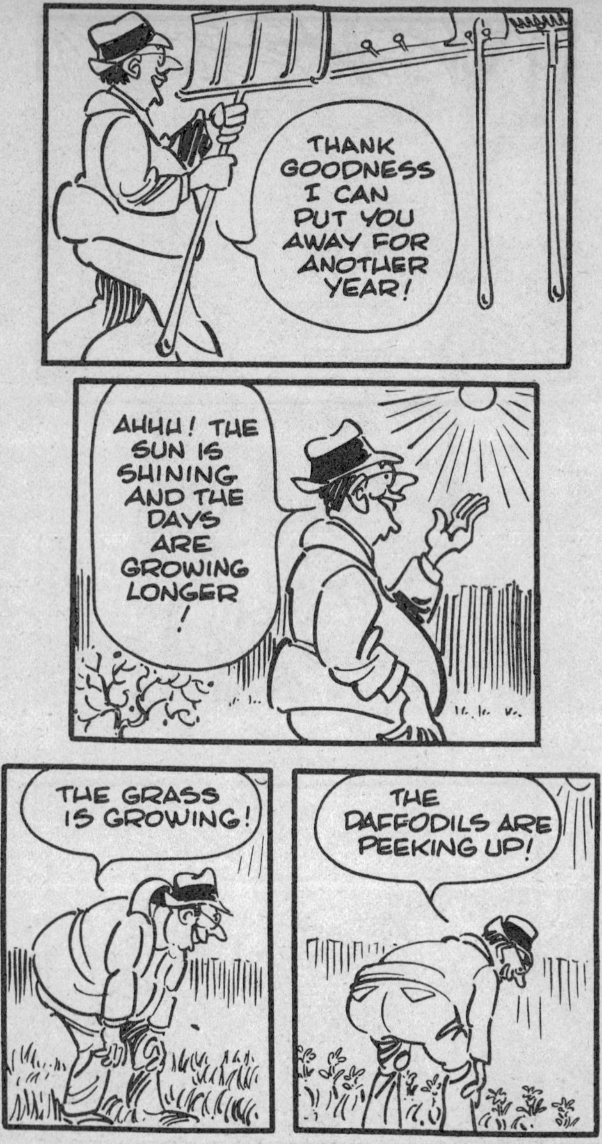
THANK GOODNESS I CAN PUT YOU AWAY FOR ANOTHER YEAR!
AHHH! THE SUN IS SHINING AND THE DAYS ARE GROWING LONGER!
THE GRASS IS GROWING!
THE DAFFODILS ARE PEEKING UP!

THE BIRDS ARE RETURNING !
AND THERE IS A SURE SIGN...
3-21
© 1982 United Feature Syndicate, Inc.
SPRING IS JUST AROUND THE CORNER !

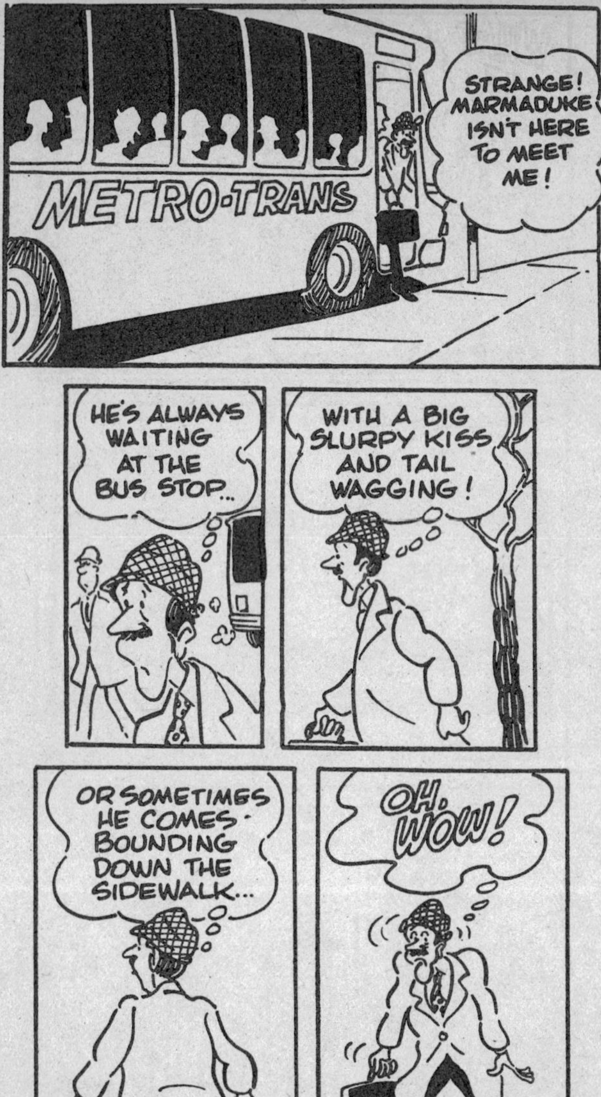
METRO-TRANS
STRANGE! MARMADUKE ISN'T HERE TO MEET ME!
HE'S ALWAYS WAITING AT THE BUS STOP...
WITH A BIG SLURPY KISS AND TAIL WAGGING!
OR SOMETIMES HE COMES BOUNDING DOWN THE SIDEWALK...
OH, WOW!

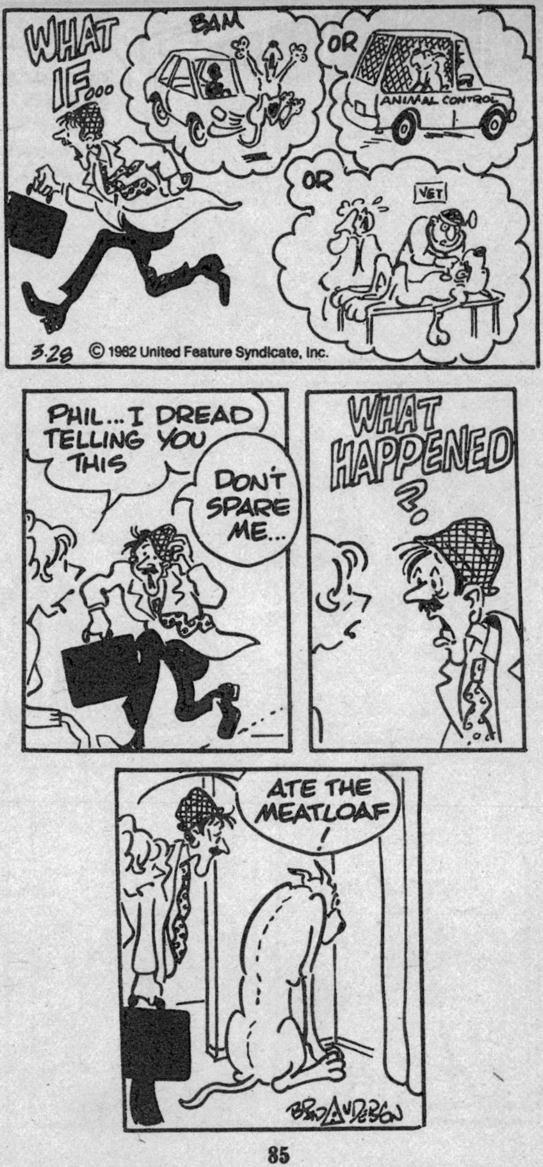
WHAT IF...
BAM
OR
ANIMAL CONTROL
OR
VET
3·28 © 1982 United Feature Syndicate, Inc.
PHIL... I DREAD TELLING YOU THIS
DON'T SPARE ME...
WHAT HAPPENED?
ATE THE MEATLOAF!

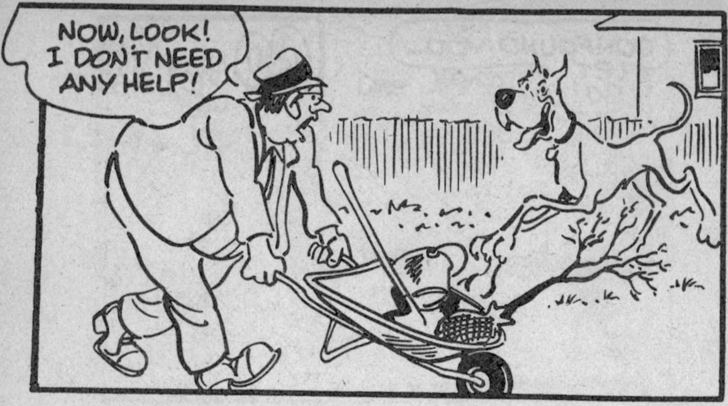
NOW, LOOK! I DON'T NEED ANY HELP!
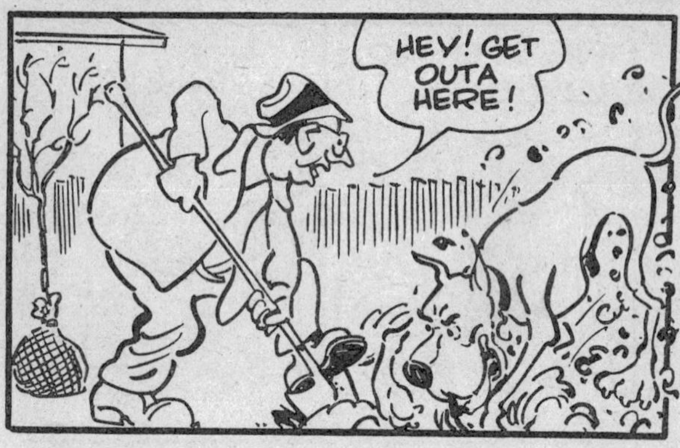
HEY! GET OUTA HERE!
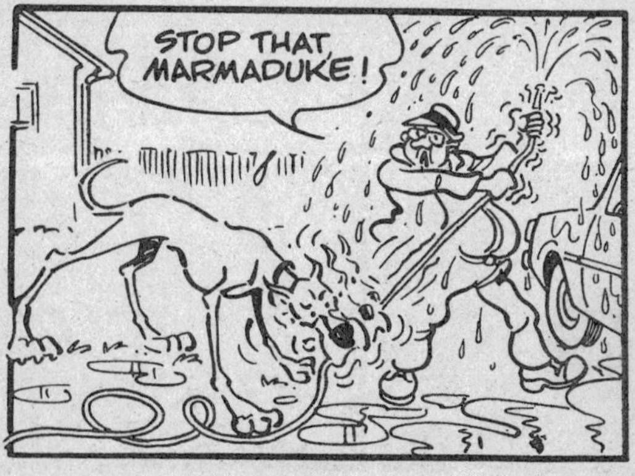
STOP THAT, MARMADUKE!

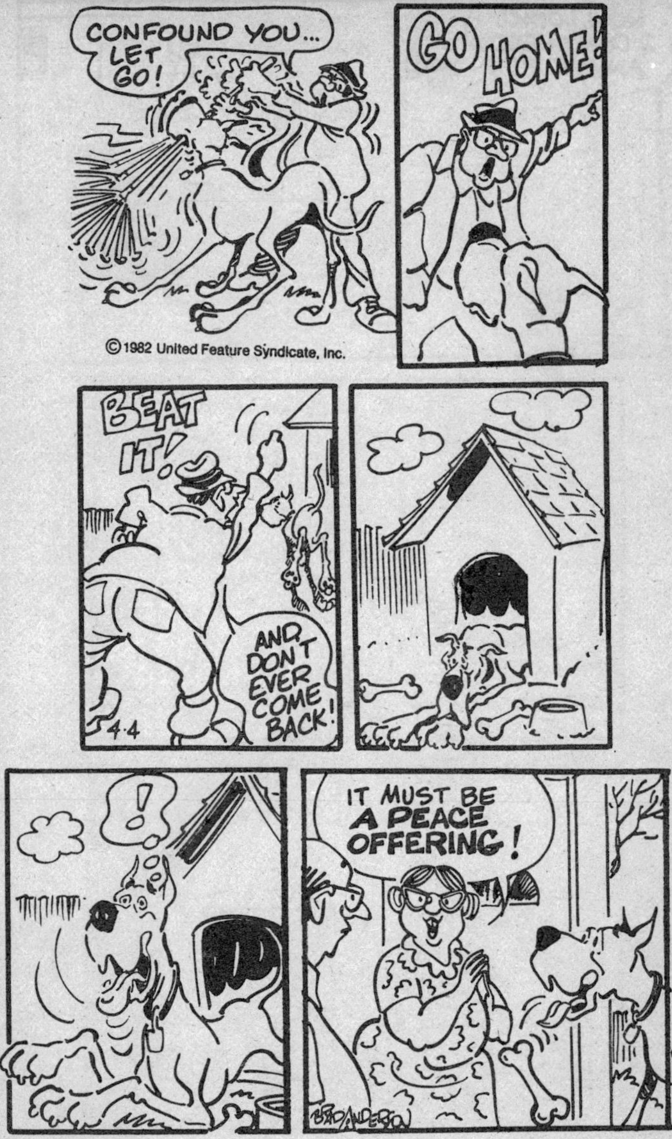
CONFOUND YOU... LET GO!
GO HOME!
BEAT IT!
AND DON'T EVER COME BACK!
4·4
!
IT MUST BE A PEACE OFFERING!
BRAD ANDERSON

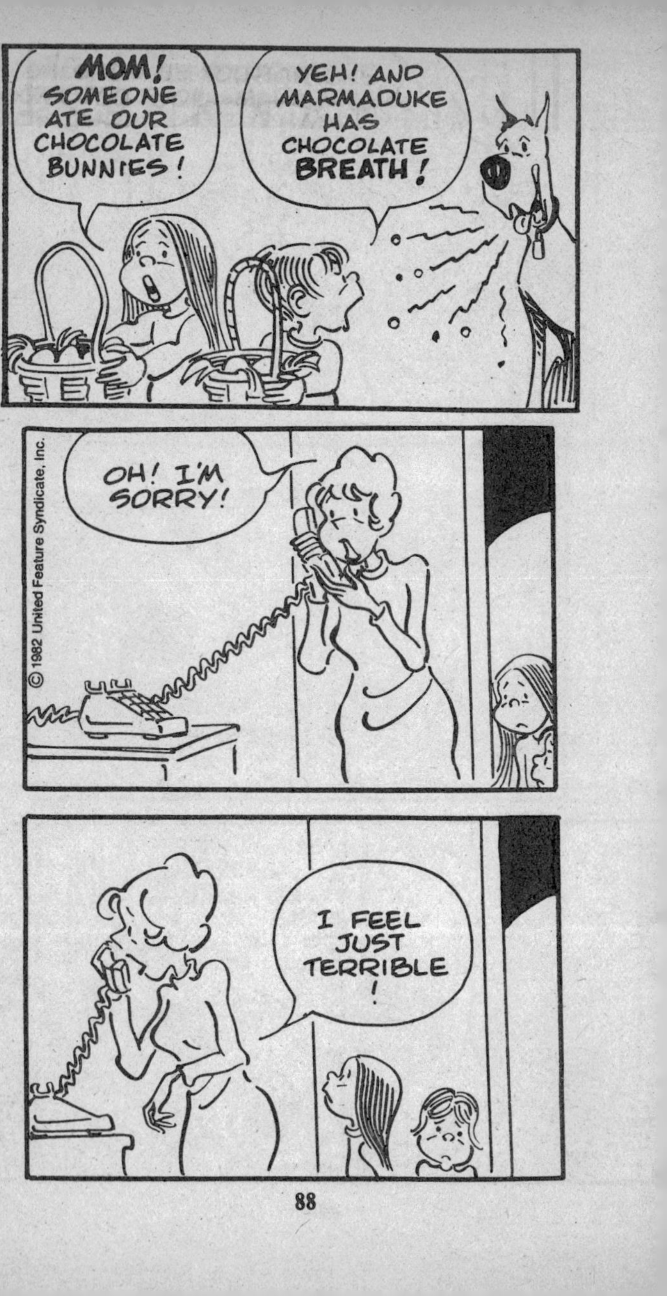
MOM! SOMEONE ATE OUR CHOCOLATE BUNNIES!
YEH! AND MARMADUKE HAS CHOCOLATE BREATH!
OH! I'M SORRY!
© 1982 United Feature Syndicate, Inc.
I FEEL JUST TERRIBLE!

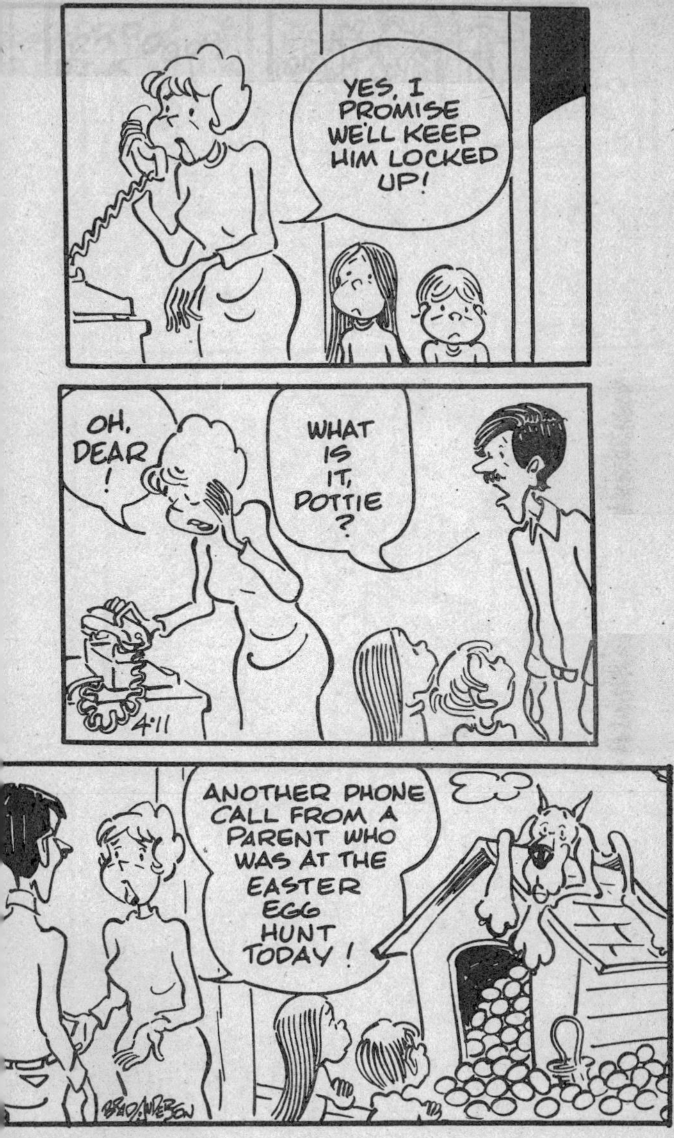
YES, I PROMISE WE'LL KEEP HIM LOCKED UP!
OH, DEAR!
WHAT IS IT, DOTTIE?
4·11
ANOTHER PHONE CALL FROM A PARENT WHO WAS AT THE EASTER EGG HUNT TODAY!
BRAD ANDERSON

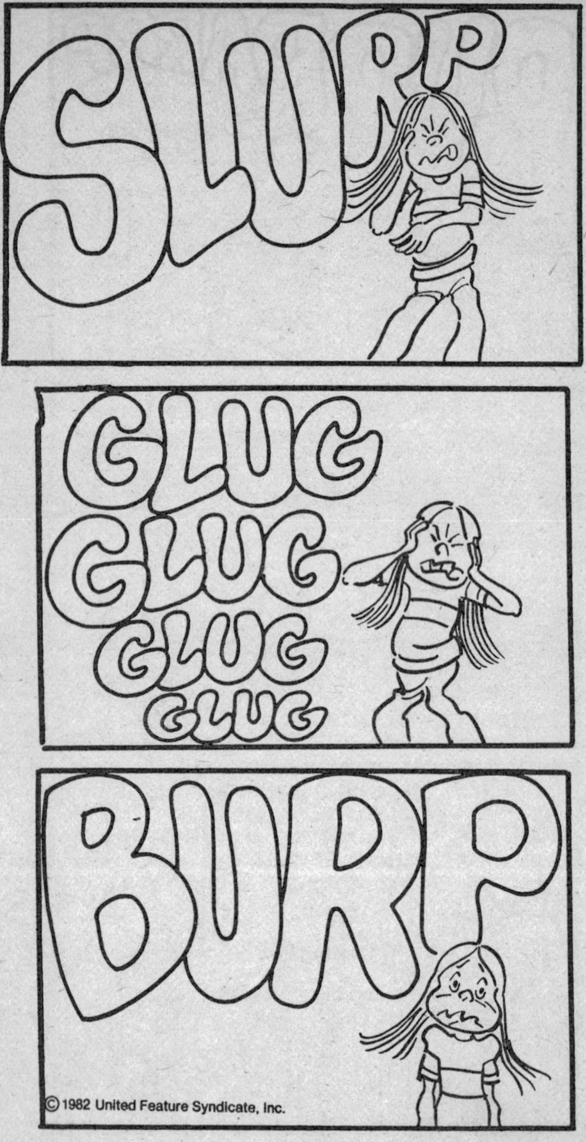
SLURP
GLUG
GLUG
GLUG
GLUG
BURP
© 1982 United Feature Syndicate, Inc.

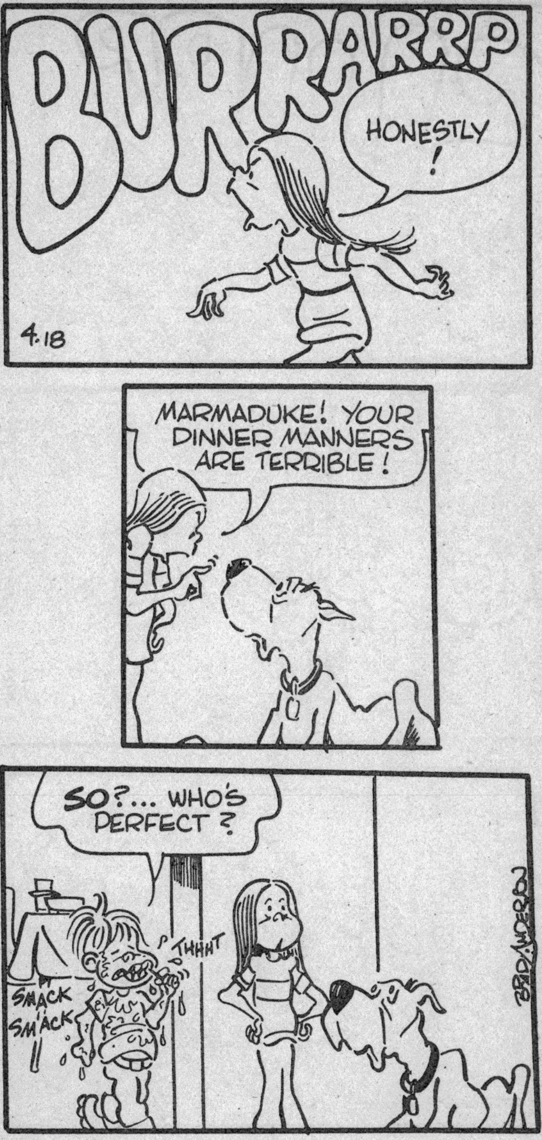
BURRARRP
HONESTLY!
4.18
MARMADUKE! YOUR DINNER MANNERS ARE TERRIBLE!
SO?... WHO'S PERFECT?
THHHT
SMACK
SMACK
BRAD ANDERSON

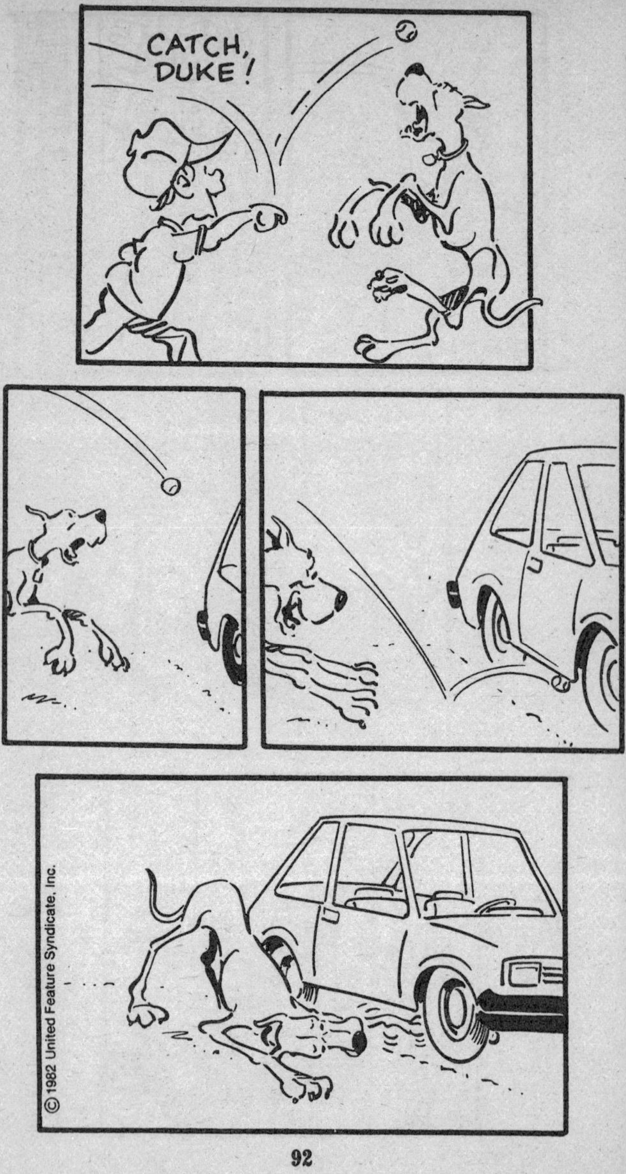
CATCH, DUKE!

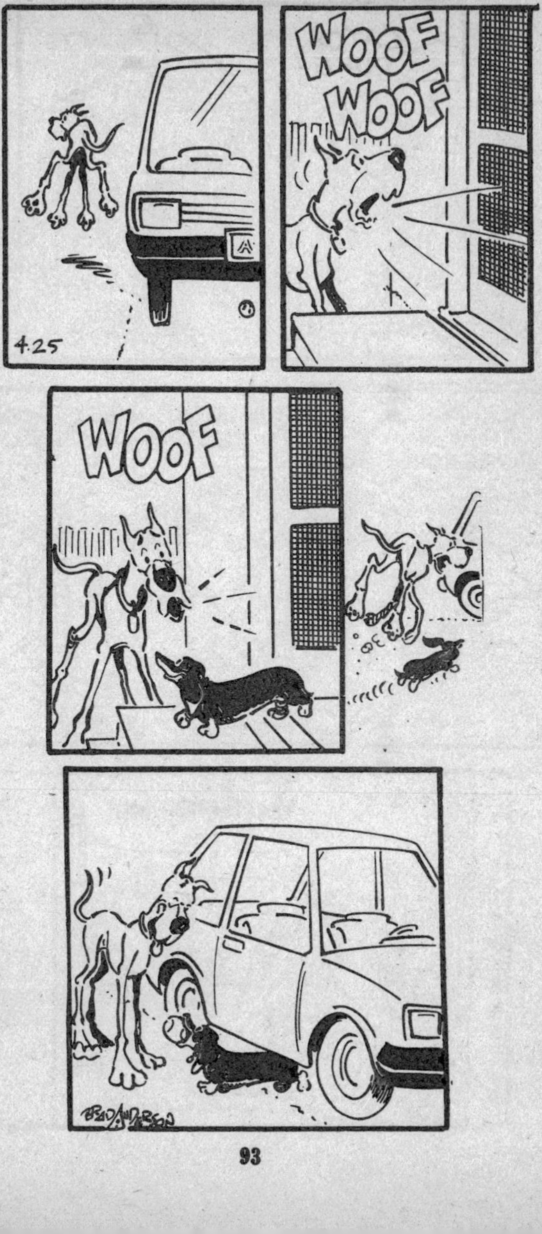
4.25
WOOF WOOF
WOOF
BRAD ANDERSON

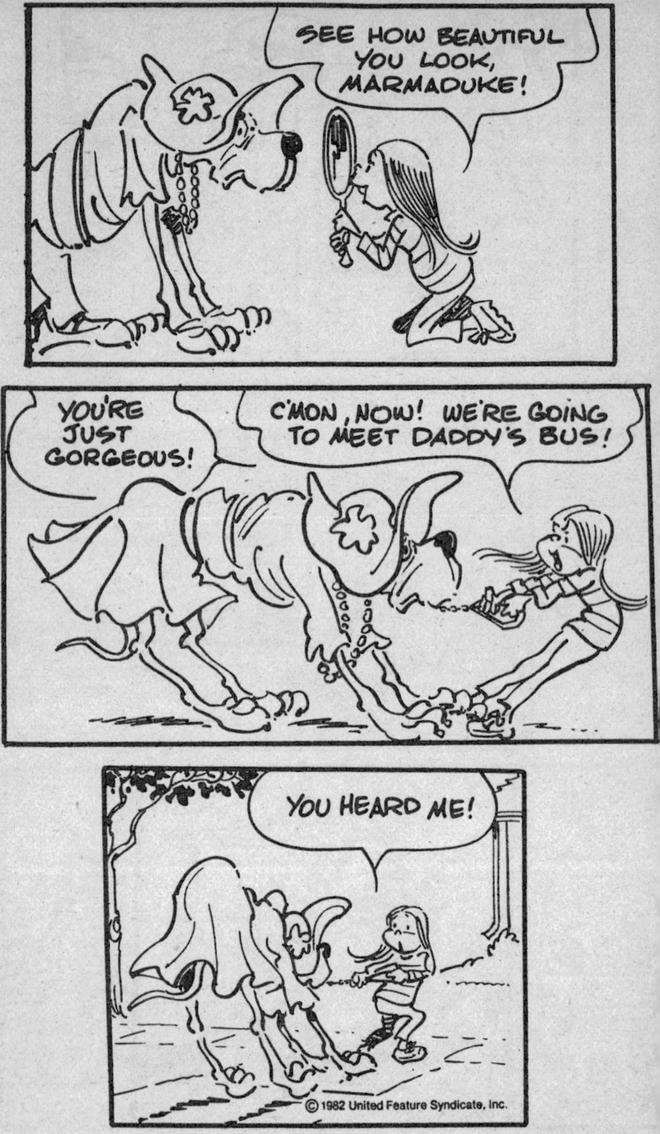
SEE HOW BEAUTIFUL YOU LOOK, MARMADUKE!
YOU'RE JUST GORGEOUS!
C'MON, NOW! WE'RE GOING TO MEET DADDY'S BUS!
YOU HEARD ME!
© 1982 United Feature Syndicate, Inc.

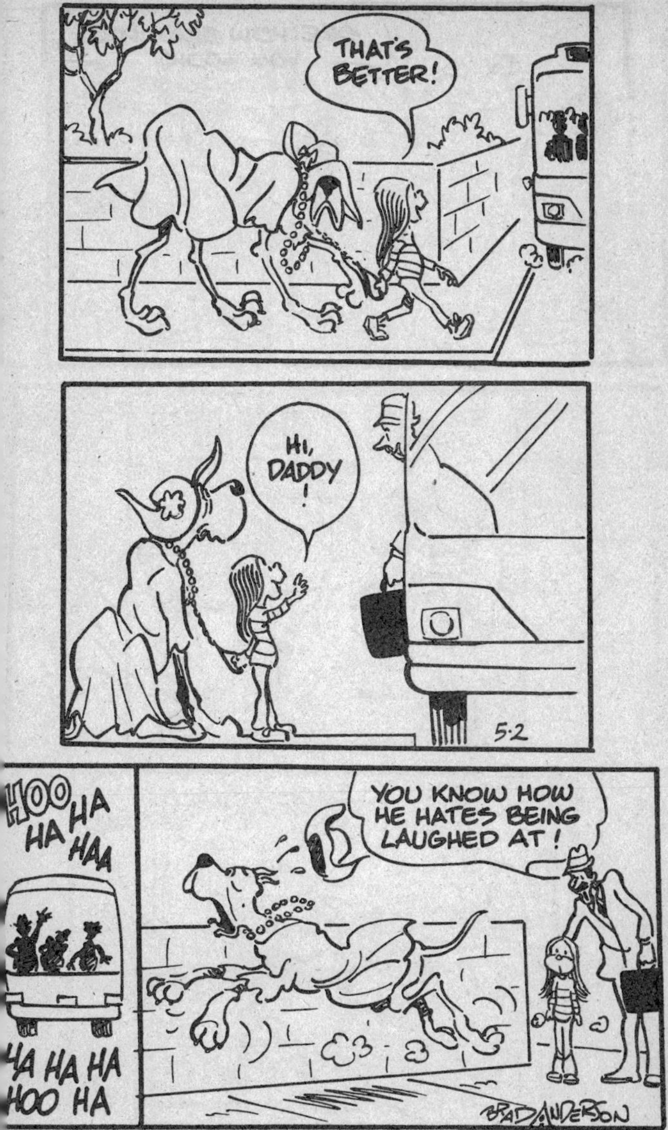
THAT'S BETTER!
HI, DADDY!
5·2
HOO HA HA HAA
HA HA HA HOO HA
YOU KNOW HOW HE HATES BEING LAUGHED AT!
BRAD ANDERSON

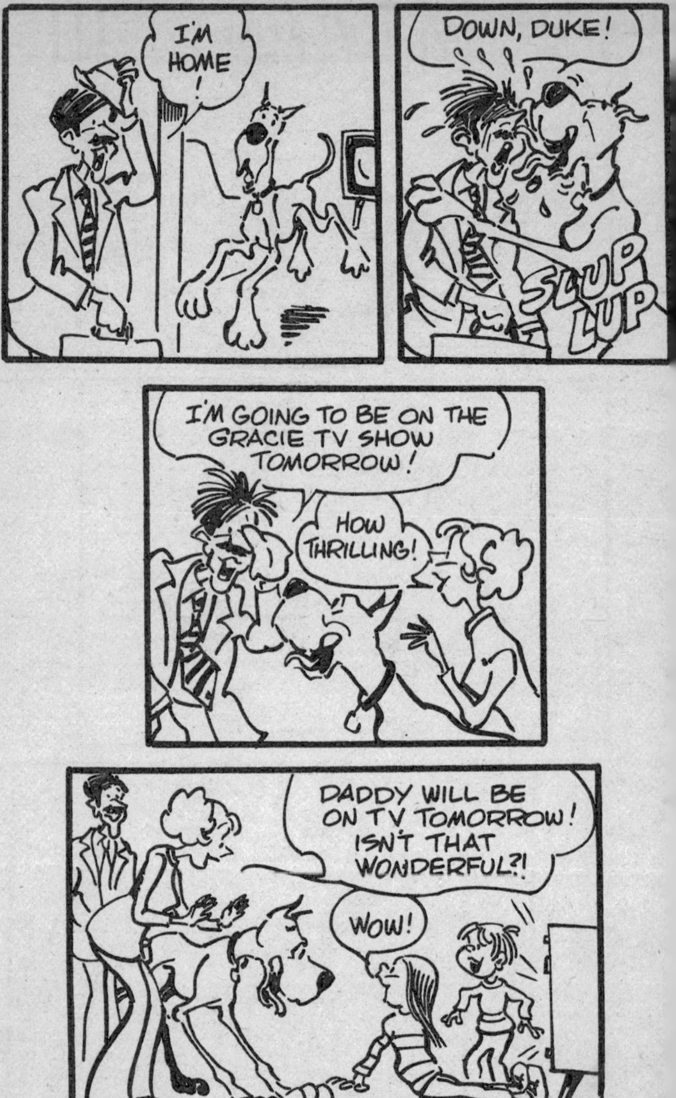
I'M HOME!
DOWN, DUKE!
SLUP LUP
I'M GOING TO BE ON THE GRACIE TV SHOW TOMORROW!
HOW THRILLING!
DADDY WILL BE ON TV TOMORROW! ISN'T THAT WONDERFUL?!
WOW!

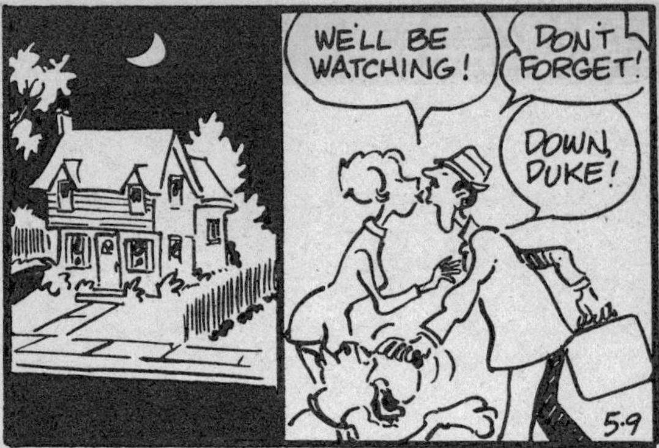
WE'LL BE WATCHING!
DON'T FORGET!
DOWN, DUKE!
5-9

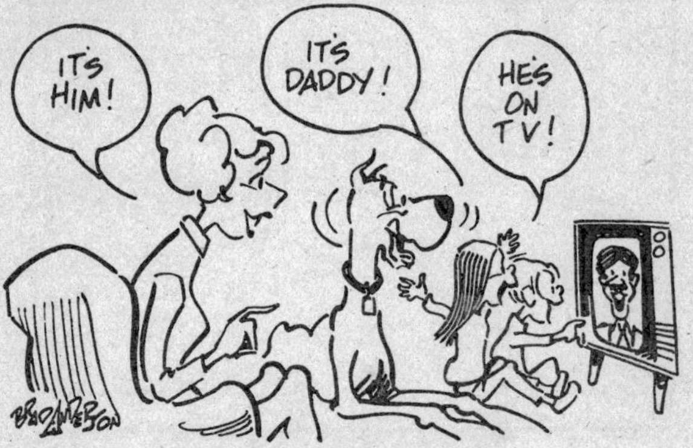
IT'S HIM!
IT'S DADDY!
HE'S ON TV!

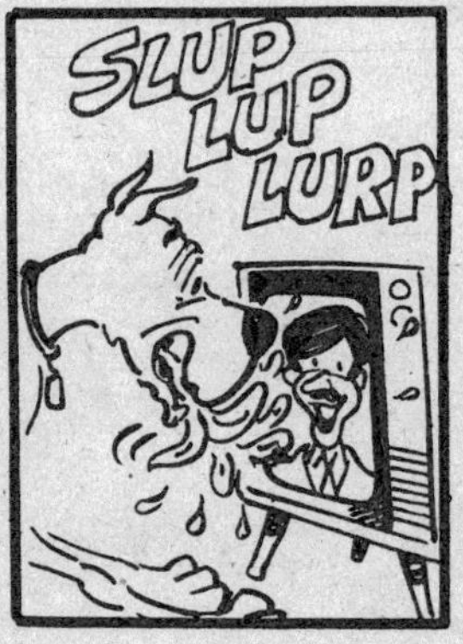
SLUP LUP LURP

MMRRUM

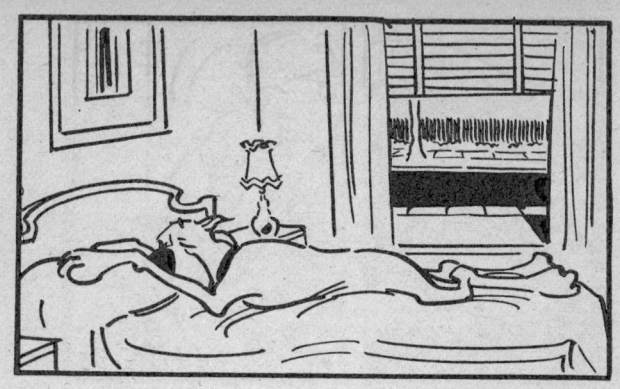

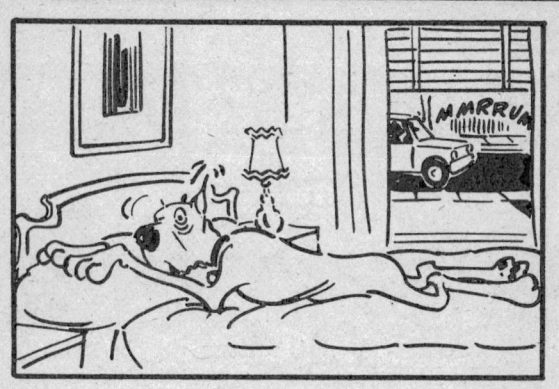

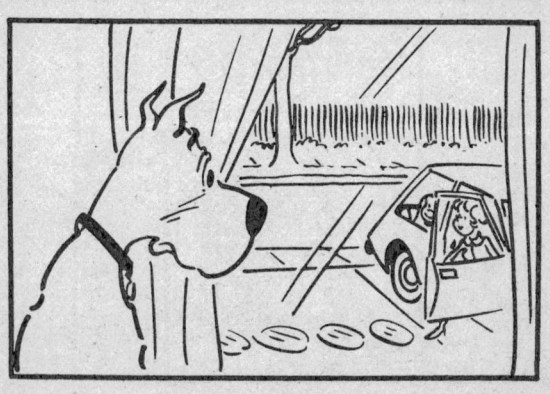

5·16
SHHH...LET'S SURPRISE DUKE!
BRAD ANDERSON

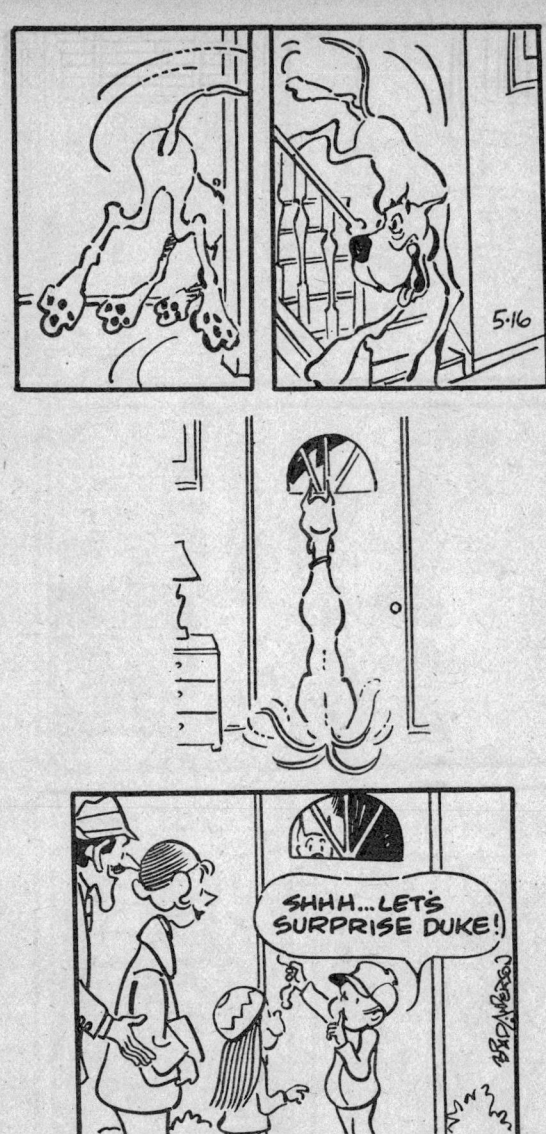

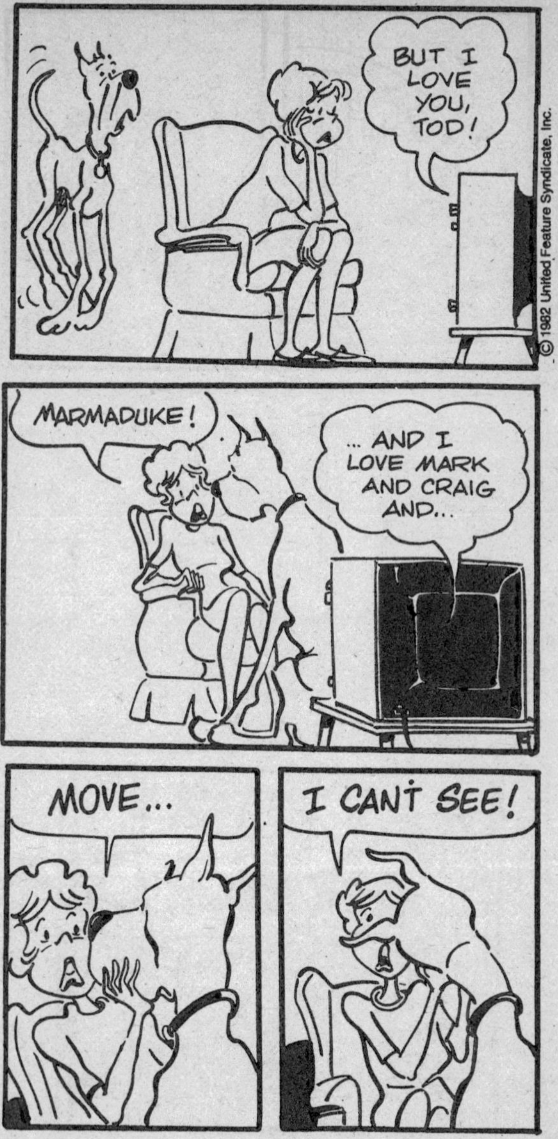
BUT I LOVE YOU, TOD!
© 1982 United Feature Syndicate, Inc.
MARMADUKE!
... AND I LOVE MARK AND CRAIG AND...
MOVE...
I CAN'T SEE!

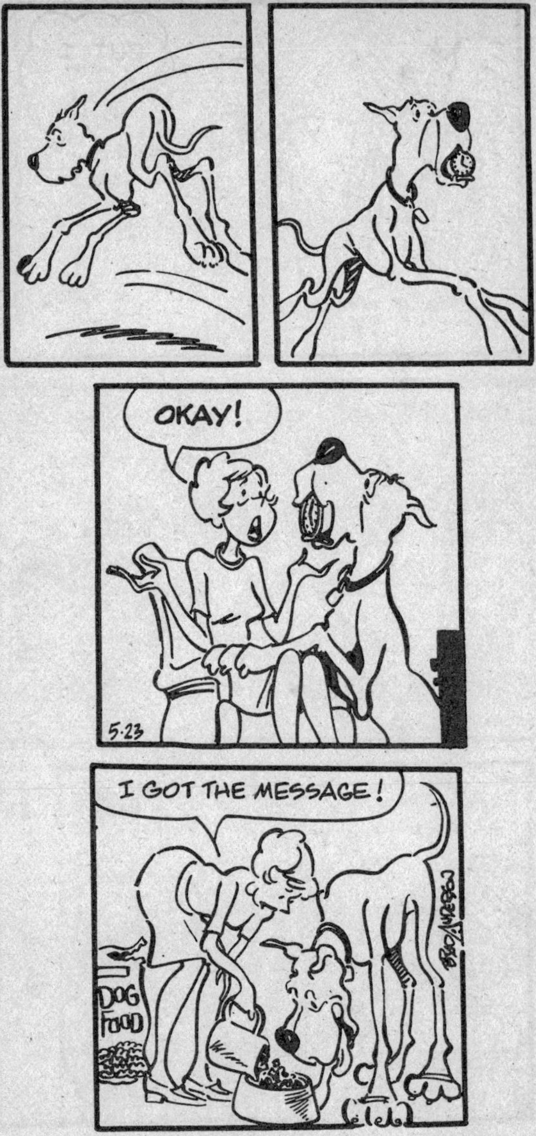
OKAY!
5·23
I GOT THE MESSAGE!
DOG FOOD
BRAD ANDERSON

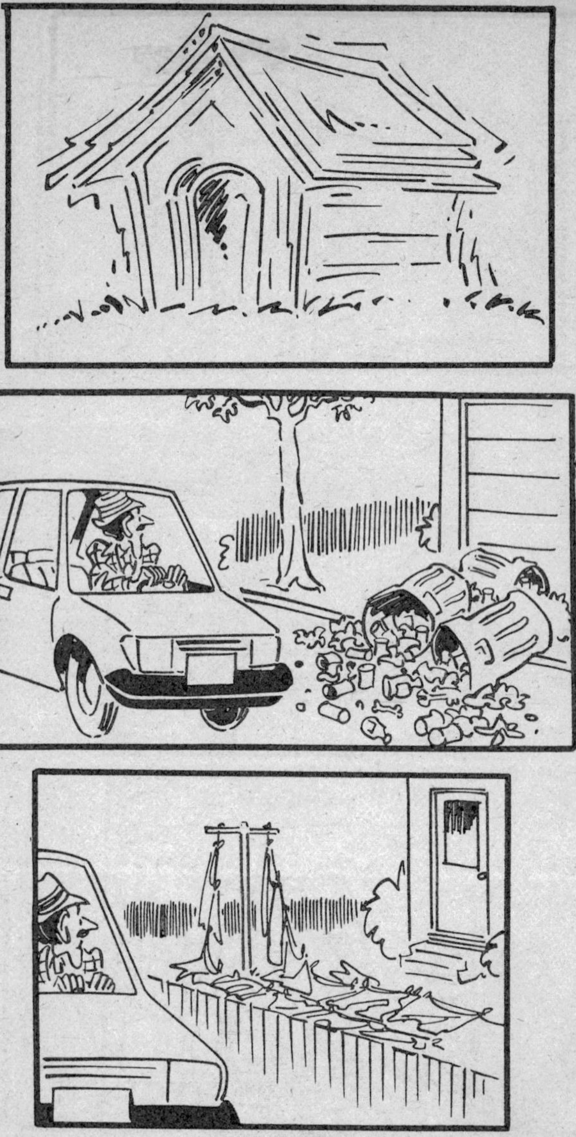

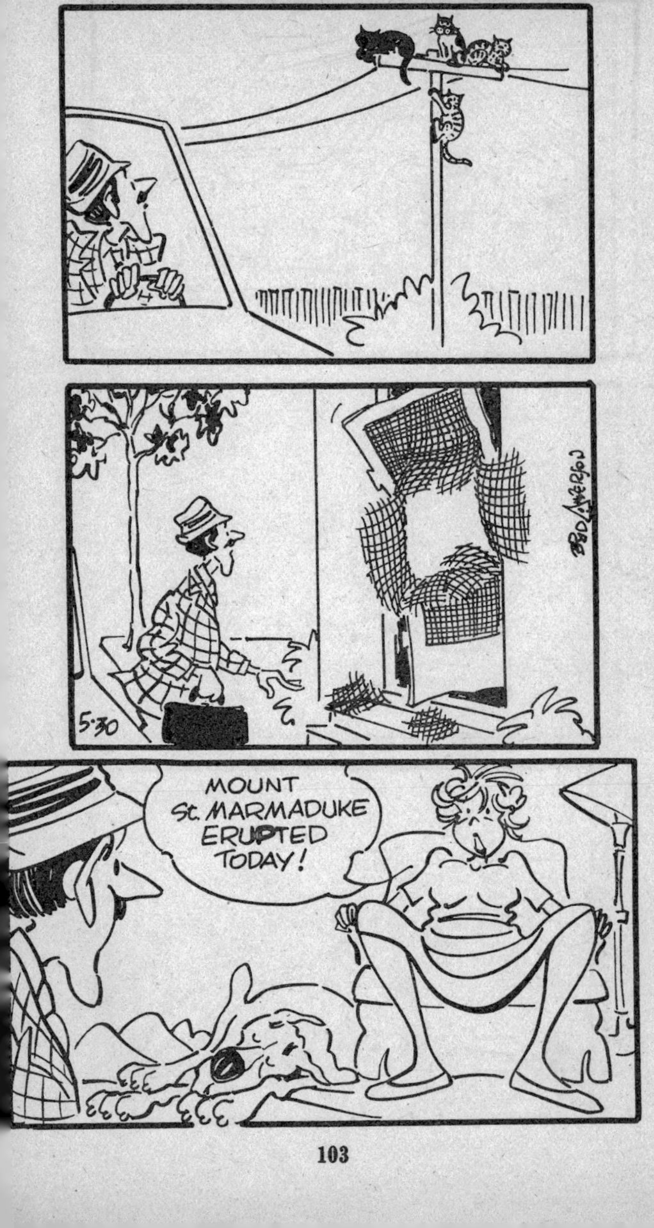
5·30
MOUNT St. MARMADUKE ERUPTED TODAY!

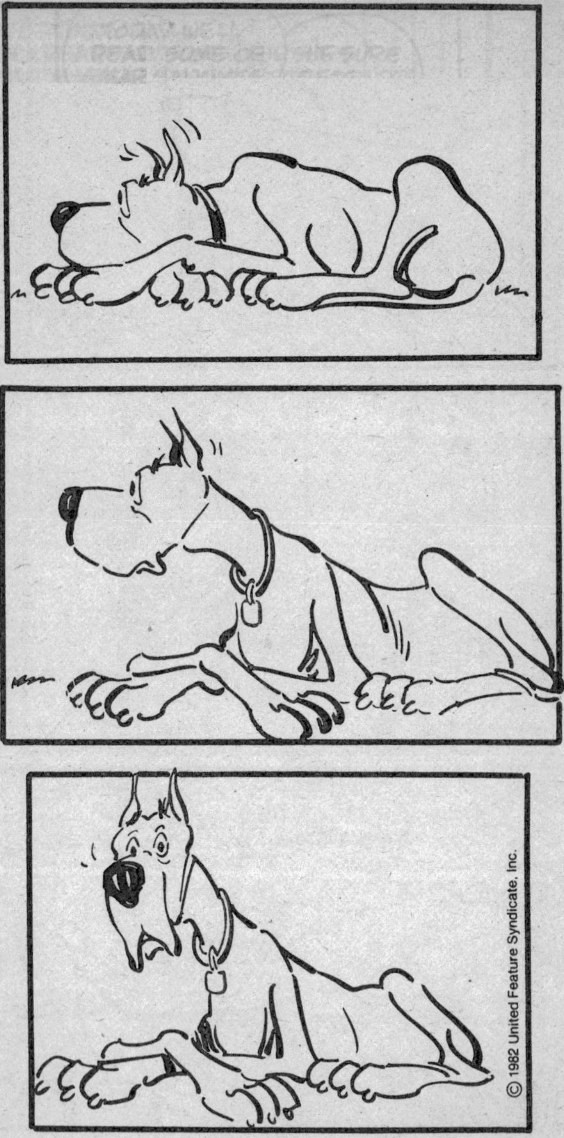

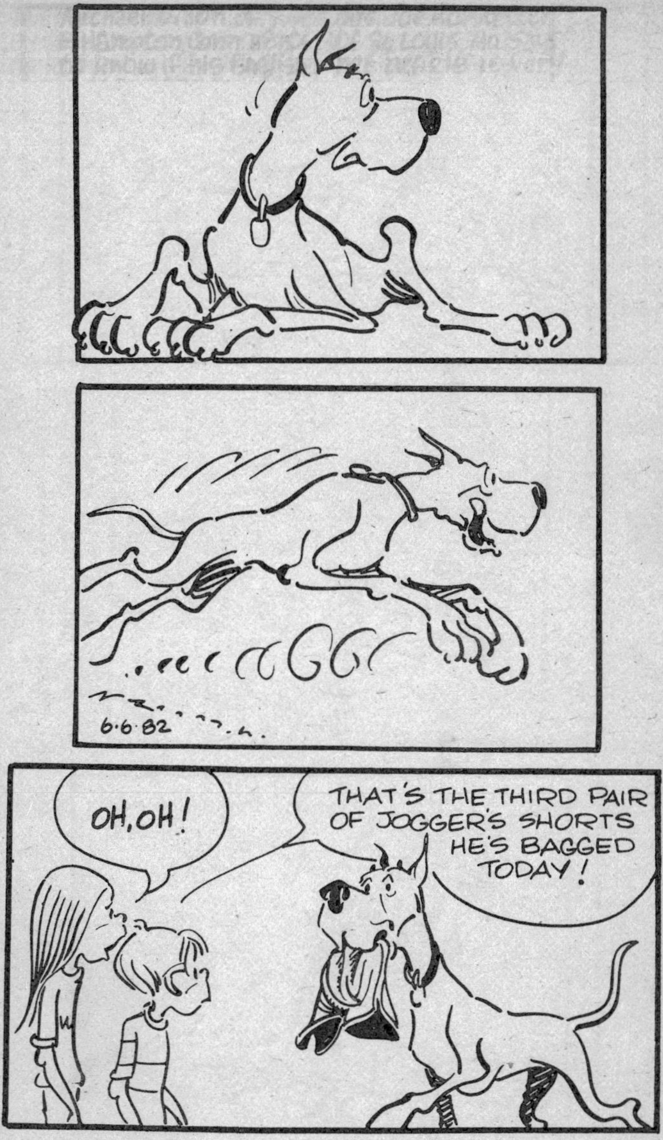
6·6·82
OH, OH!
THAT'S THE THIRD PAIR OF JOGGER'S SHORTS HE'S BAGGED TODAY!

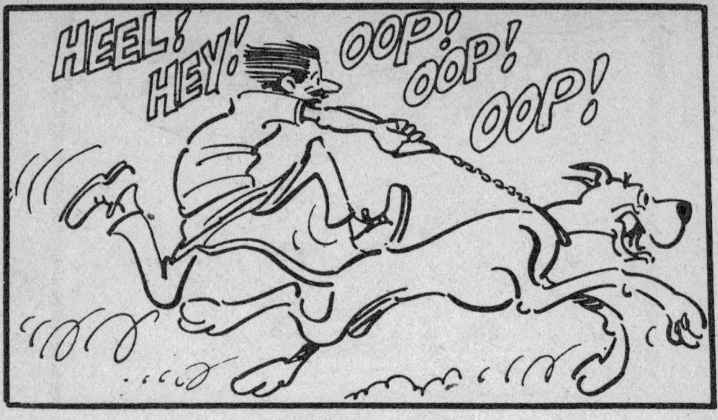
HEEL! HEY!
OOP! OOP! OOP!

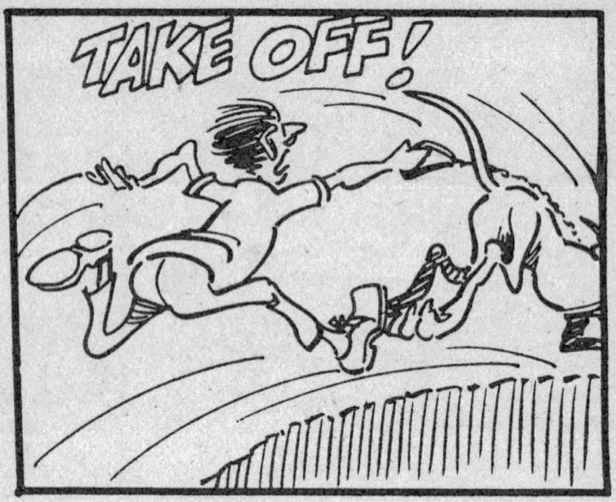
TAKE OFF!

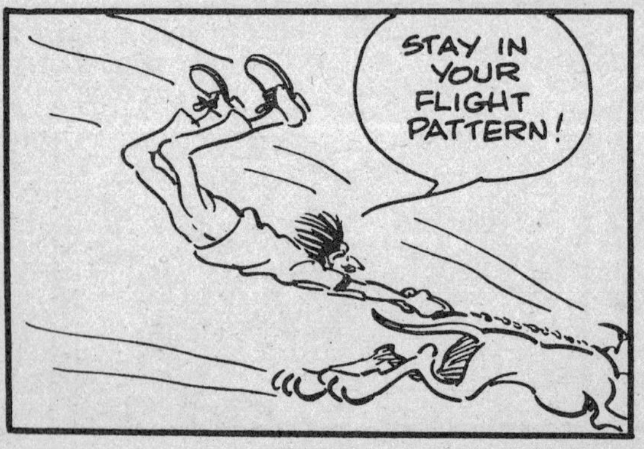
STAY IN YOUR FLIGHT PATTERN!

LOWER FLAPS
6·13
LANDING GEAR DOWN
HE'S CURED ME! I'M OVER MY FEAR OF FLYING!
BRAD ANDERSON
© 1982 United Feature Syndicate, Inc.

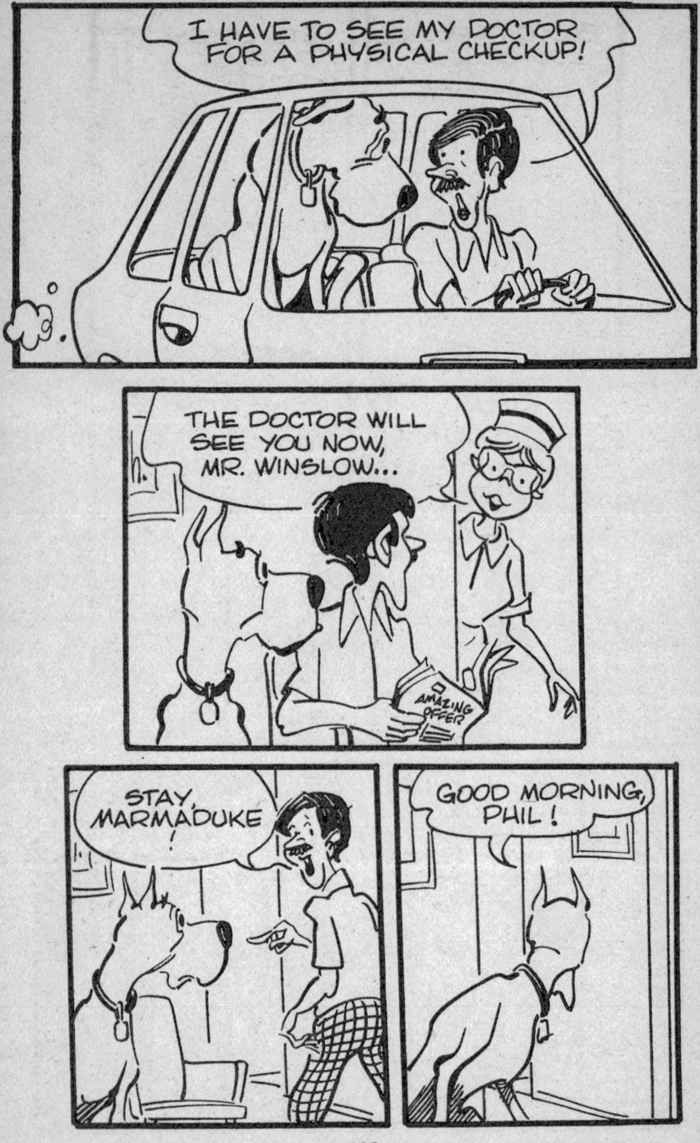
I HAVE TO SEE MY DOCTOR FOR A PHYSICAL CHECKUP!
THE DOCTOR WILL SEE YOU NOW, MR. WINSLOW...
AMAZING OFFER
STAY, MARMADUKE!
GOOD MORNING, PHIL!

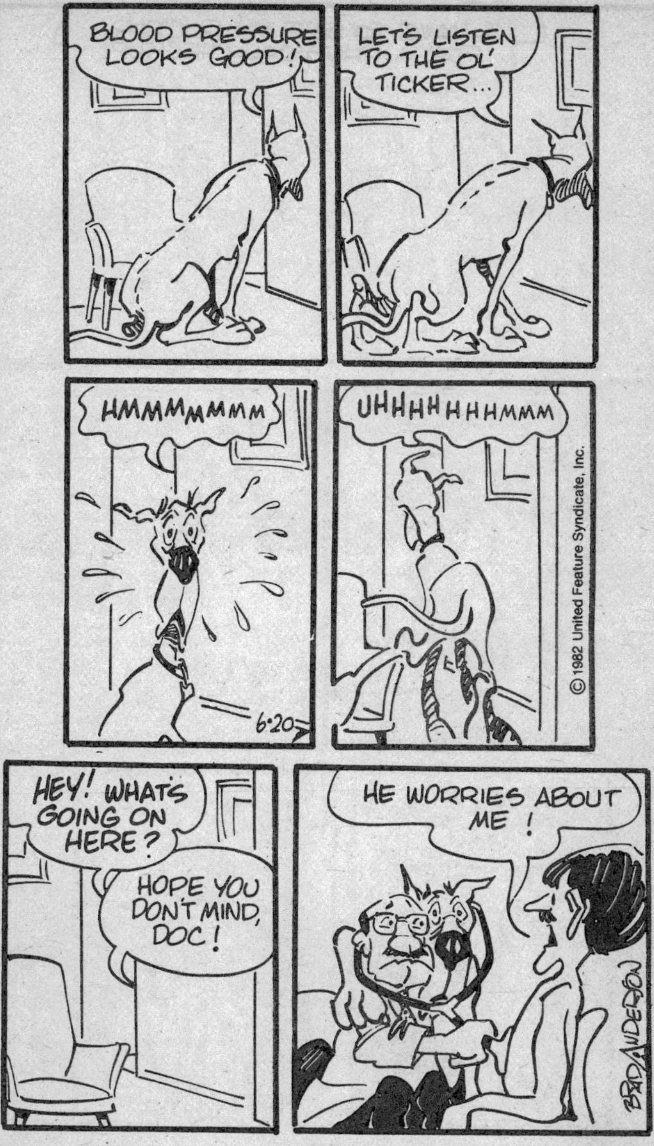
BLOOD PRESSURE LOOKS GOOD!
LET'S LISTEN TO THE OL' TICKER...
HMMMMMMMM
6·20
UHHHHHHHMMM
© 1982 United Feature Syndicate, Inc.
HEY! WHAT'S GOING ON HERE?
HOPE YOU DON'T MIND, DOC!
HE WORRIES ABOUT ME!
BRAD ANDERSON

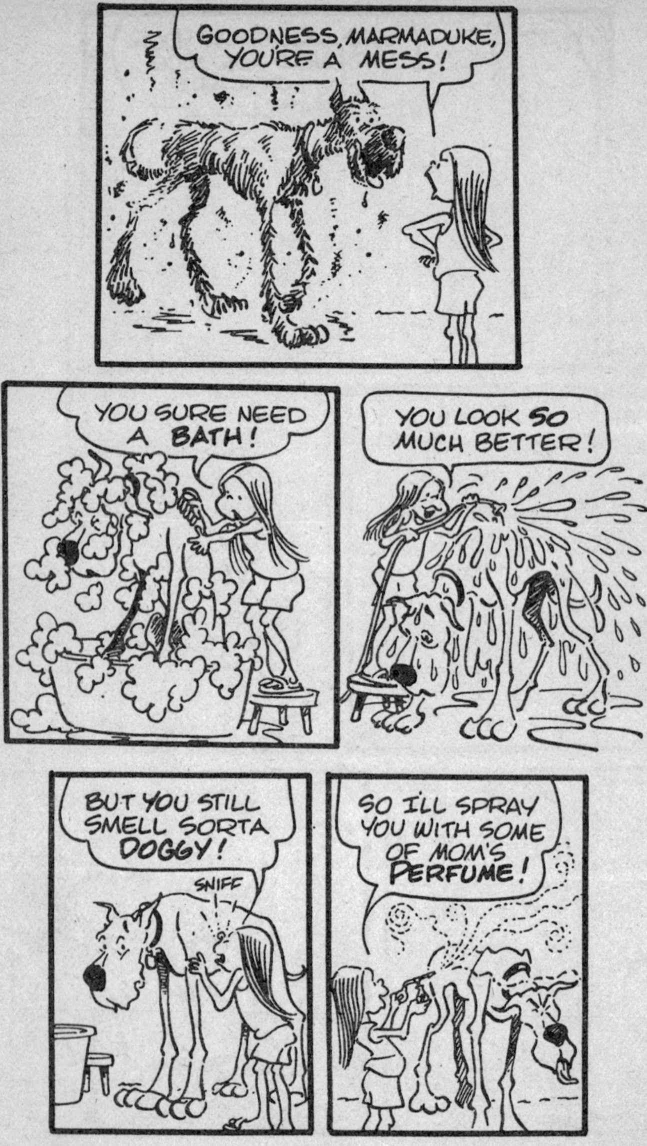
GOODNESS, MARMADUKE, YOU'RE A MESS!
YOU SURE NEED A BATH!
YOU LOOK SO MUCH BETTER!
BUT YOU STILL SMELL SORTA DOGGY!
SNIFF
SO I'LL SPRAY YOU WITH SOME OF MOM'S PERFUME!

AND WE'LL SHOW YOUR FRIENDS HOW NICE YOU LOOK AND SMELL!
© 1982 United Feature Syndicate, Inc.
6·27
SNIFF SNIFF SNIFF SNIFF SNIFF SNIFF SNIFF SNIFF SNIFF SNIFF
HONESTLY, MARMADUKE... YOU'RE HOPELESS!
B.A.

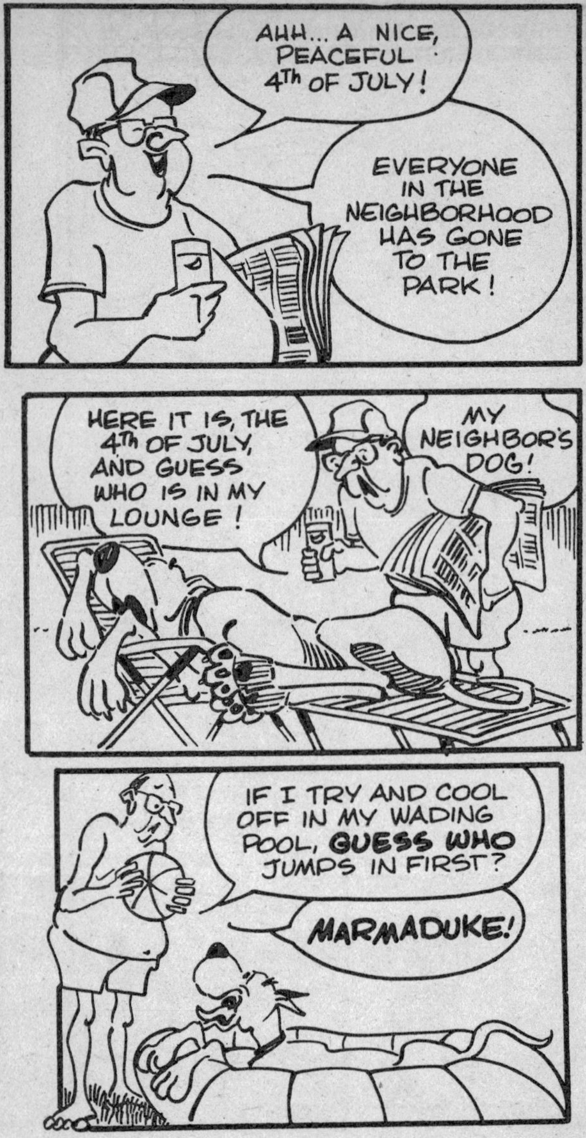
AHH... A NICE, PEACEFUL 4th OF JULY!
EVERYONE IN THE NEIGHBORHOOD HAS GONE TO THE PARK!
HERE IT IS, THE 4th OF JULY, AND GUESS WHO IS IN MY LOUNGE!
MY NEIGHBOR'S DOG!
IF I TRY AND COOL OFF IN MY WADING POOL, GUESS WHO JUMPS IN FIRST?
MARMADUKE!

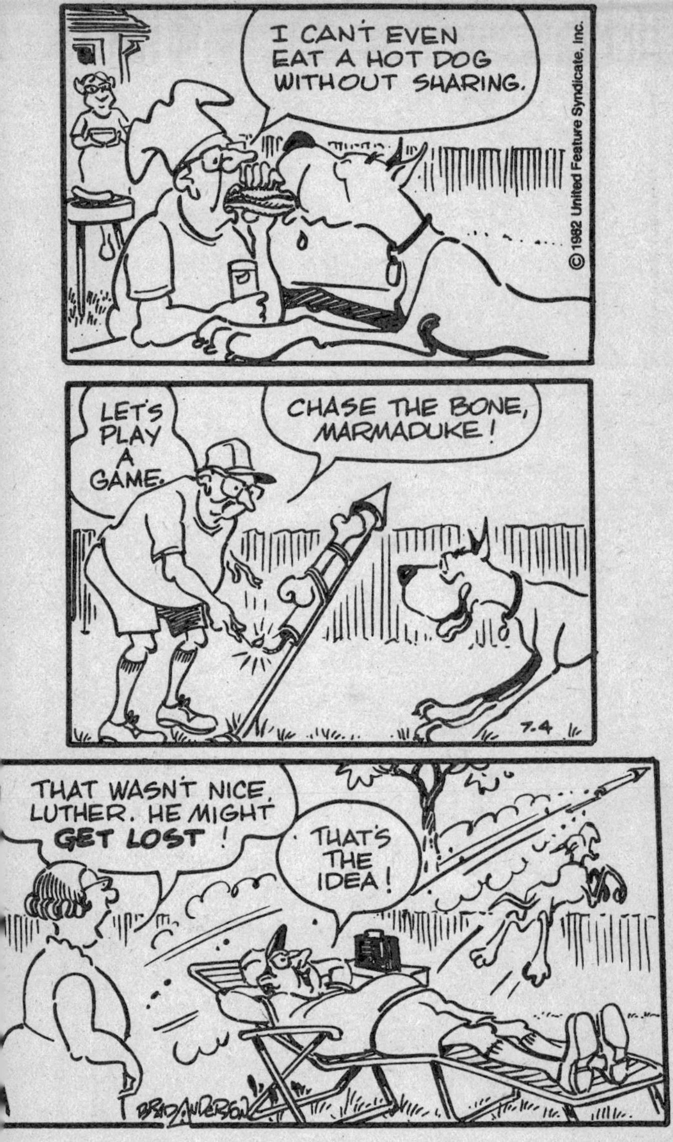
I CAN'T EVEN EAT A HOT DOG WITHOUT SHARING.
© 1982 United Feature Syndicate, Inc.
LET'S PLAY A GAME.
CHASE THE BONE, MARMADUKE!
7-4
THAT WASN'T NICE, LUTHER. HE MIGHT **GET LOST**!
THAT'S THE IDEA!
BRAD ANDERSON

FORGET IT! NO WAY YOU'RE GETTING THIS LOUNGE!
© 1982 United Feature Syndicate, Inc.

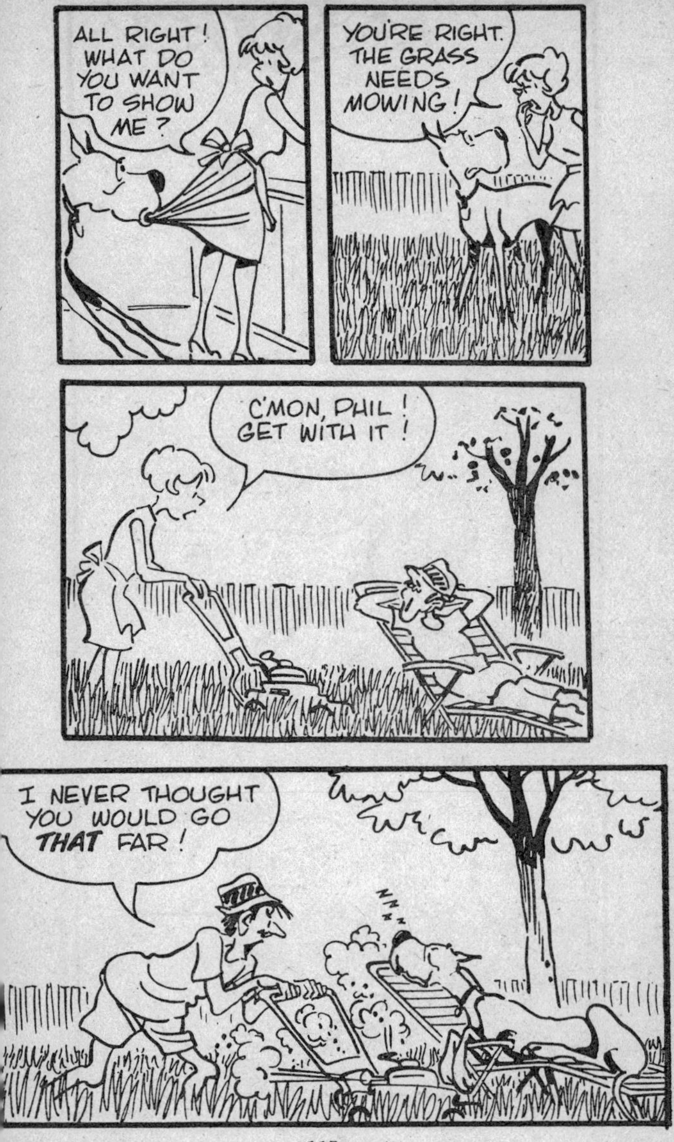
ALL RIGHT! WHAT DO YOU WANT TO SHOW ME?
YOU'RE RIGHT. THE GRASS NEEDS MOWING!
C'MON, PHIL! GET WITH IT!
I NEVER THOUGHT YOU WOULD GO **THAT** FAR!
Z Z Z Z

PURRRRRRR
PURRRRRRRRR
PURRRRRRRRR

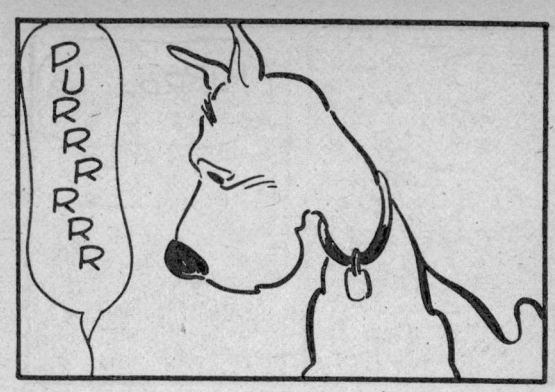

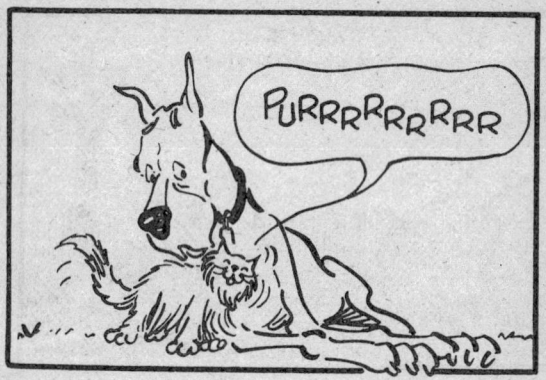

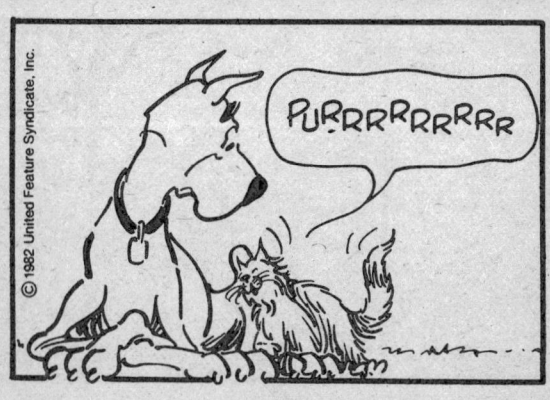

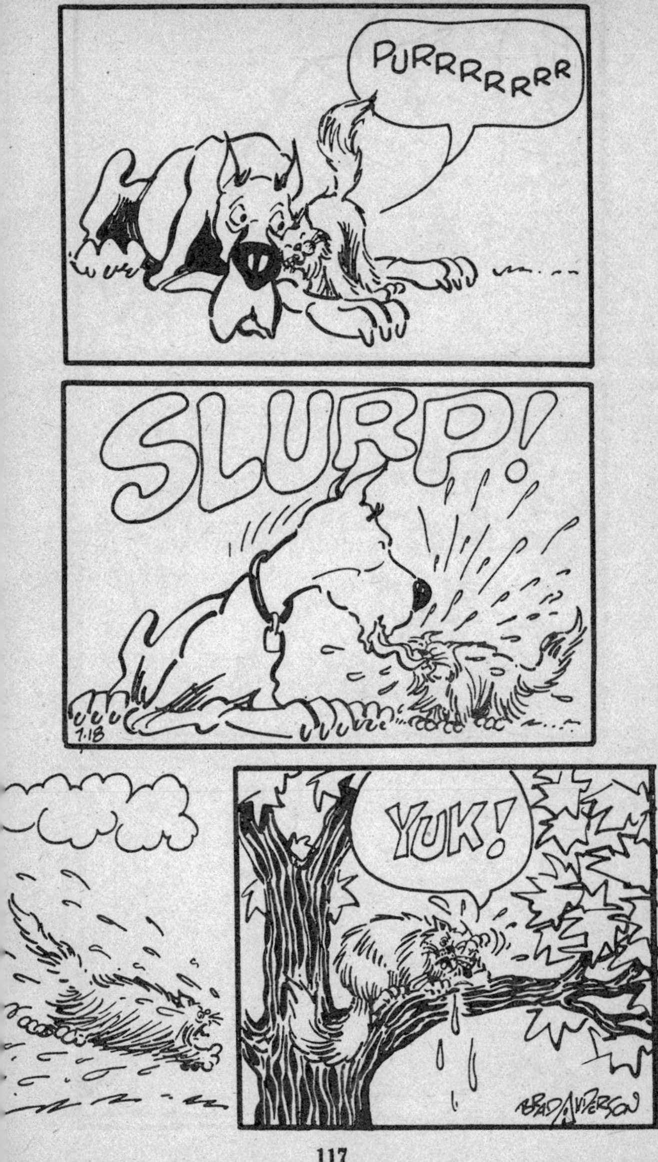
PURRRRRRRR
SLURP!
7.18
YUK!
BRAD ANDERSON

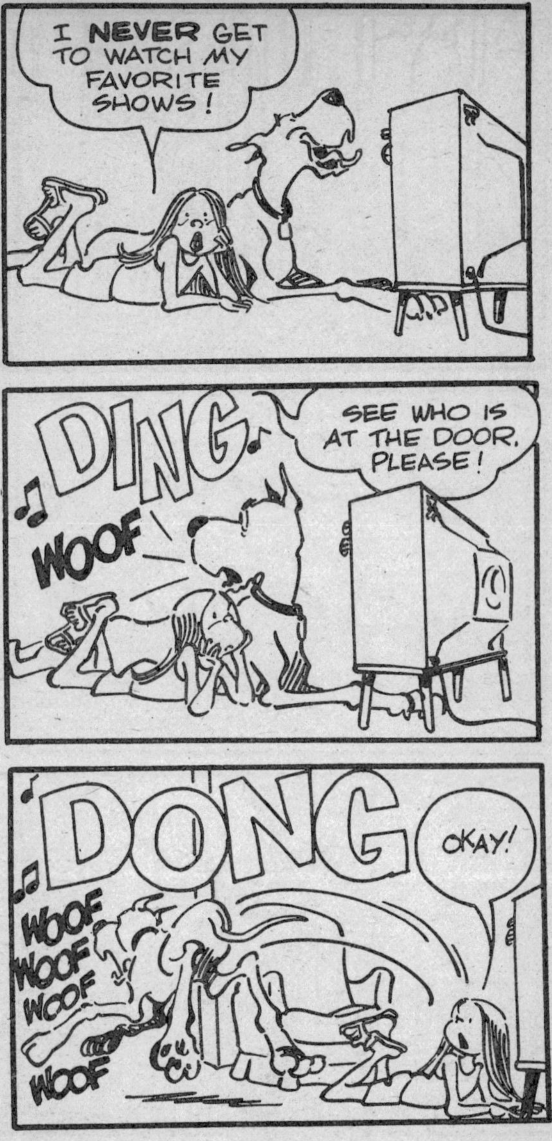
I NEVER GET TO WATCH MY FAVORITE SHOWS!
DING
WOOF
SEE WHO IS AT THE DOOR, PLEASE!
DONG
OKAY!
WOOF
WOOF
WOOF
WOOF

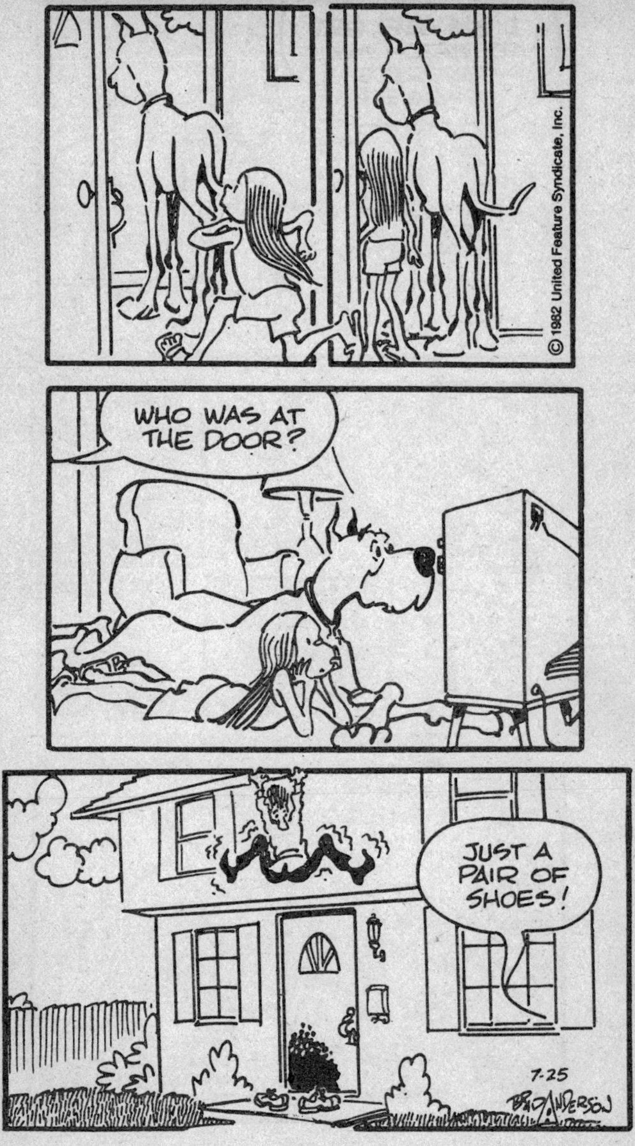

© 1982 United Feature Syndicate, Inc.
WHO WAS AT THE DOOR?
JUST A PAIR OF SHOES!
7-25
BRAD ANDERSON

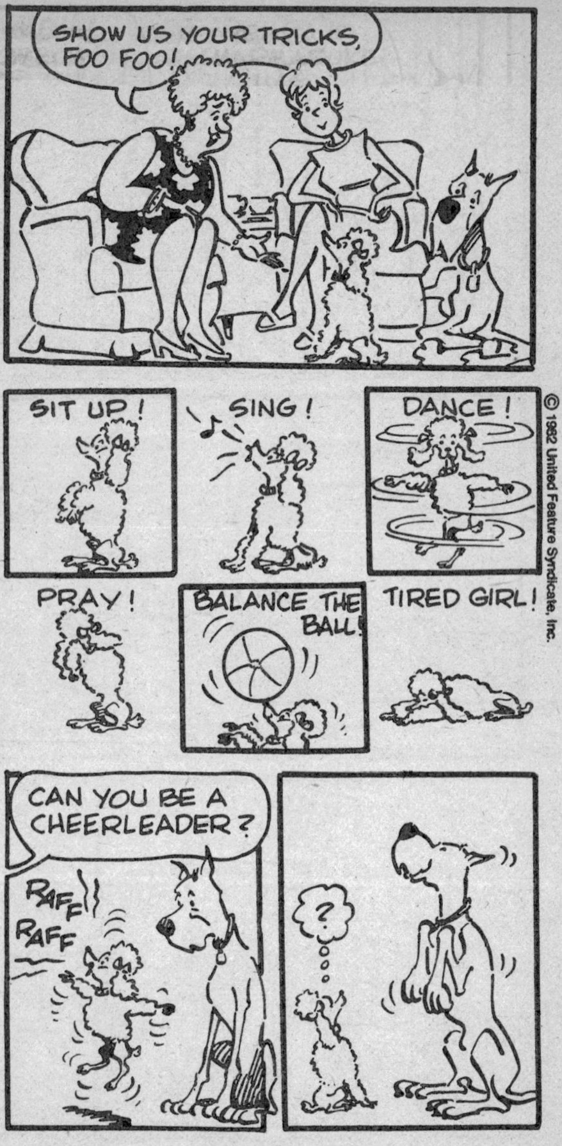
SHOW US YOUR TRICKS, FOO FOO!
SIT UP!
SING!
DANCE!
PRAY!
BALANCE THE BALL!
TIRED GIRL!
CAN YOU BE A CHEERLEADER?
RAFF
RAFF
?
© 1982 United Feature Syndicate, Inc.

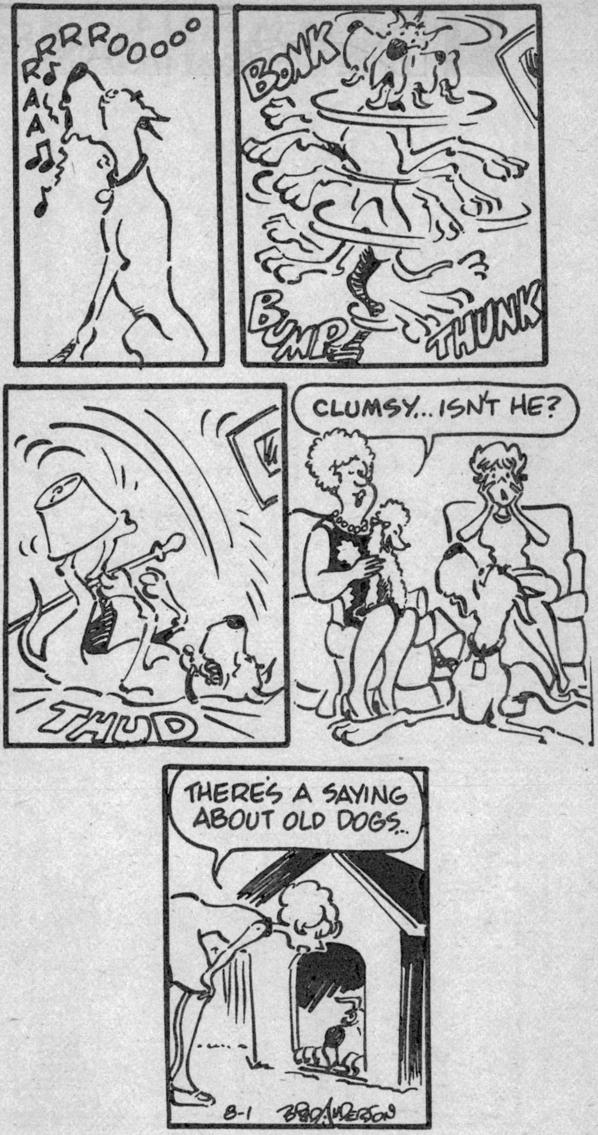
RRRRROOOOOO
AAA
BONK
BUMP
THUNK
THUD
CLUMSY... ISN'T HE?
THERE'S A SAYING ABOUT OLD DOGS...
8-1
BRAD ANDERSON

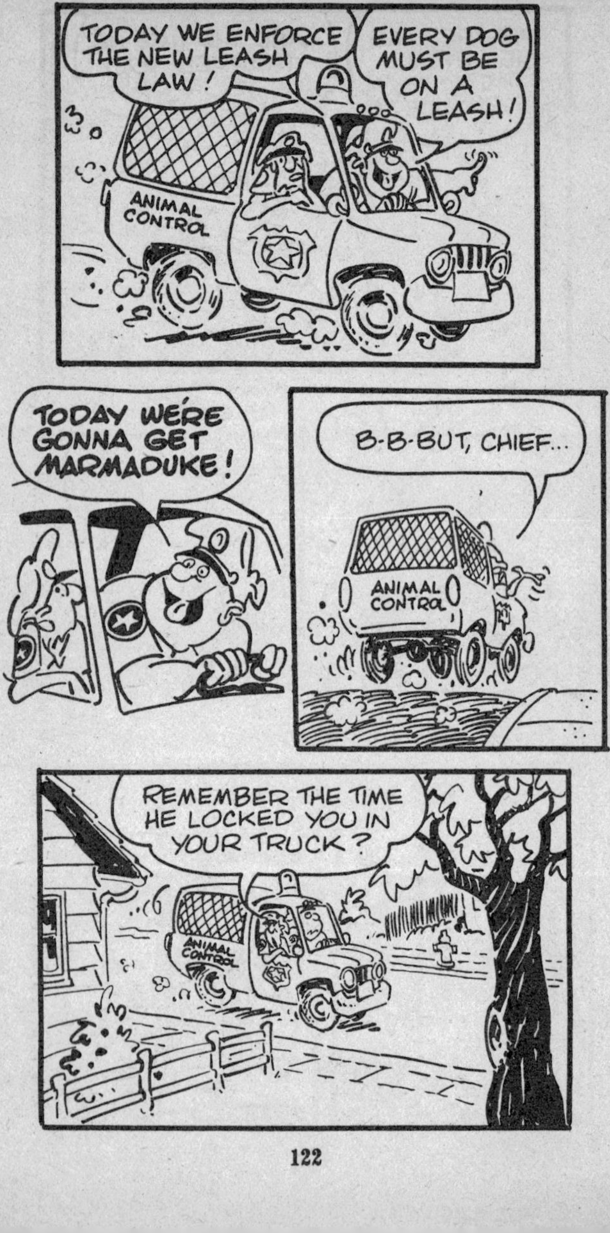
TODAY WE ENFORCE THE NEW LEASH LAW!
EVERY DOG MUST BE ON A LEASH!
ANIMAL CONTROL
TODAY WE'RE GONNA GET MARMADUKE!
B-B-BUT, CHIEF...
ANIMAL CONTROL
REMEMBER THE TIME HE LOCKED YOU IN YOUR TRUCK?
ANIMAL CONTROL

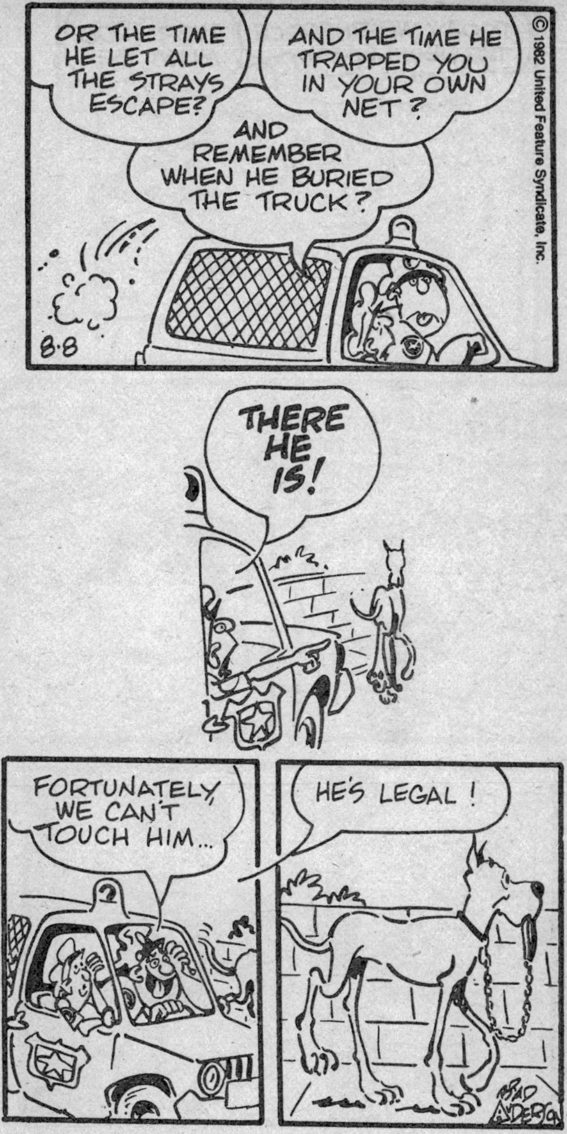
OR THE TIME HE LET ALL THE STRAYS ESCAPE?
AND THE TIME HE TRAPPED YOU IN YOUR OWN NET?
AND REMEMBER WHEN HE BURIED THE TRUCK?
© 1982 United Feature Syndicate, Inc.
8·8
THERE HE IS!
FORTUNATELY, WE CAN'T TOUCH HIM...
HE'S LEGAL!
BRAD ANDERSON

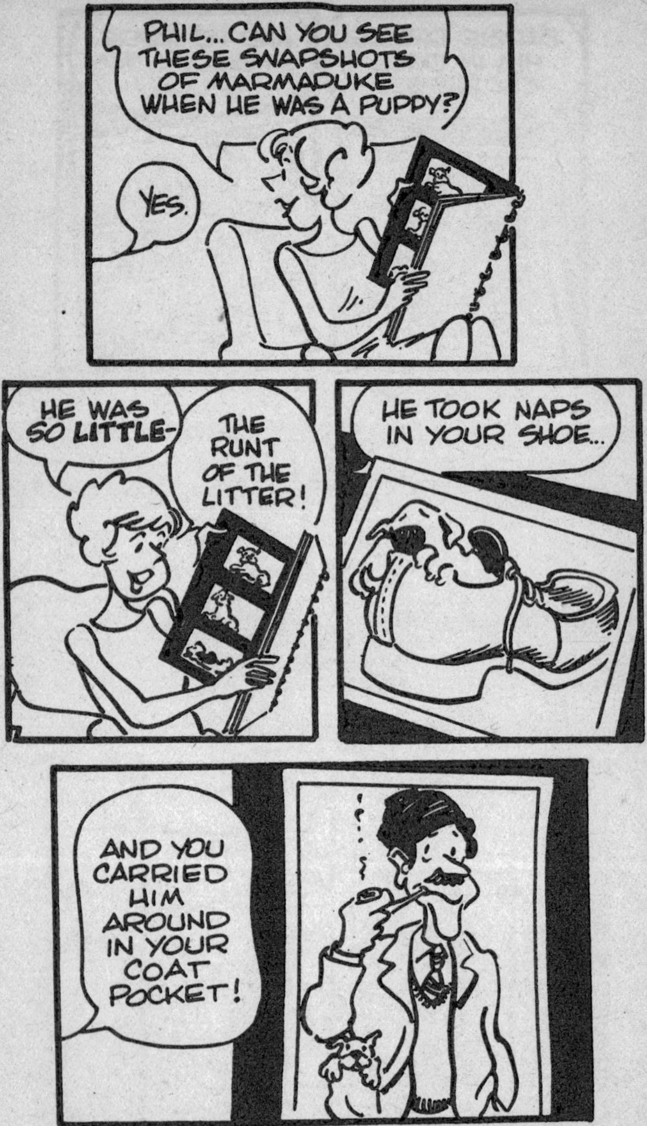
PHIL...CAN YOU SEE THESE SNAPSHOTS OF MARMADUKE WHEN HE WAS A PUPPY?
YES.
HE WAS SO LITTLE-
THE RUNT OF THE LITTER!
HE TOOK NAPS IN YOUR SHOE...
AND YOU CARRIED HIM AROUND IN YOUR COAT POCKET!

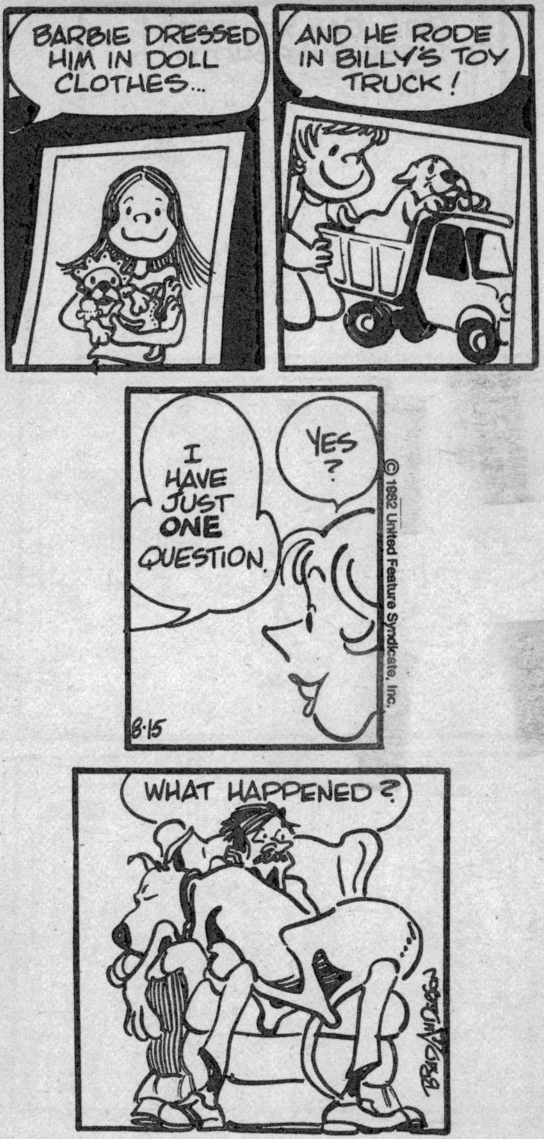
BARBIE DRESSED HIM IN DOLL CLOTHES...
AND HE RODE IN BILLY'S TOY TRUCK!
I HAVE JUST ONE QUESTION.
YES?
© 1982 United Feature Syndicate, Inc.
8·15
WHAT HAPPENED?

CRUNCH
SWAT!
SLURP!

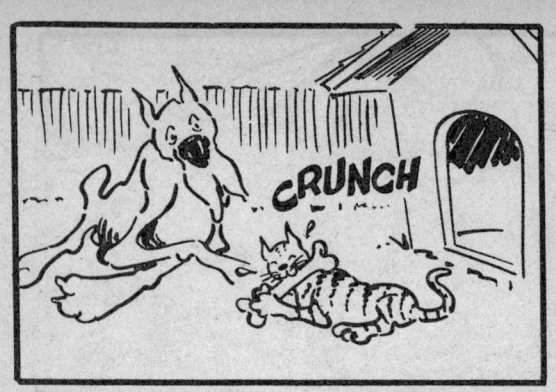

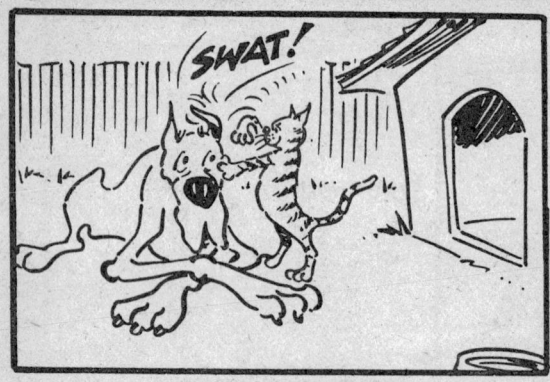

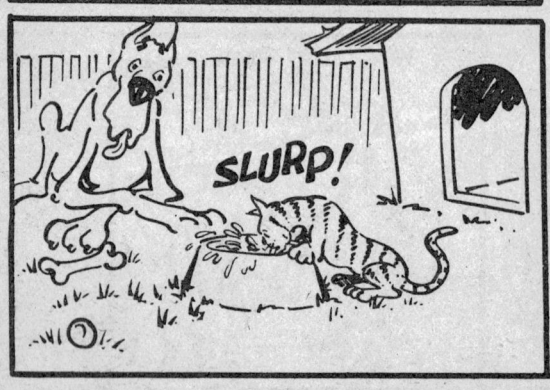

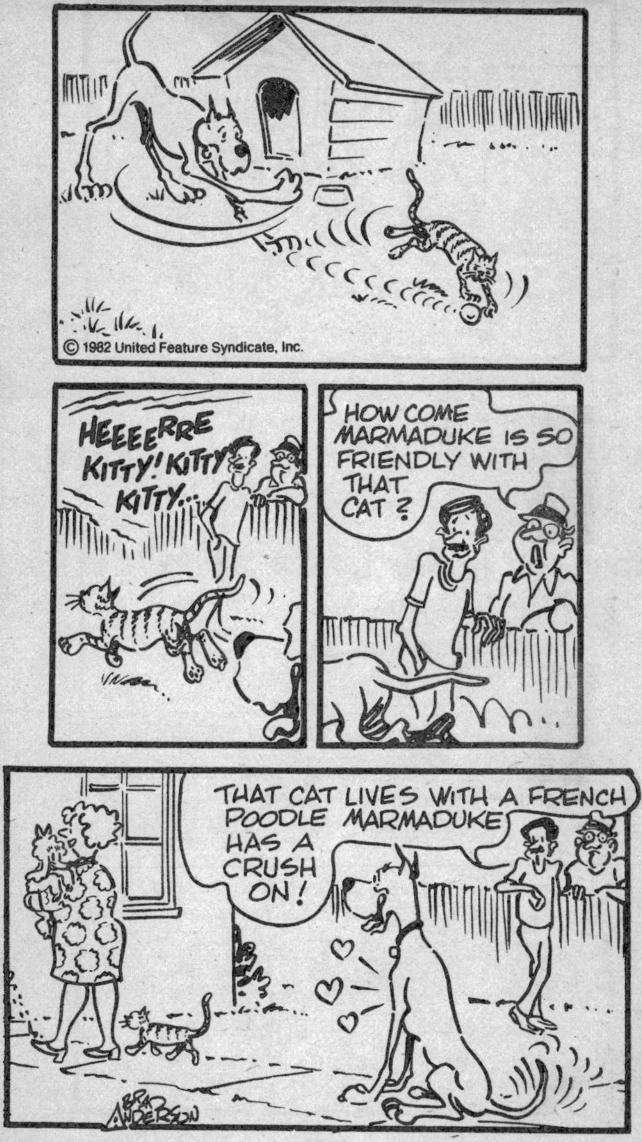
© 1982 United Feature Syndicate, Inc.
HEEEEERRRE KITTY! KITTY KITTY...
HOW COME MARMADUKE IS SO FRIENDLY WITH THAT CAT?
THAT CAT LIVES WITH A FRENCH POODLE MARMADUKE HAS A CRUSH ON!
BRAD ANDERSON

BEETLE BAILEY

THE WACKIEST G.I. IN THE ARMY

☐	56126-0	BEETLE BAILEY: WELCOME TO CAMP SWAMPY!	$3.95
☐	56127-9		Canada $4.95
☐	56109-0	BEETLE BAILEY: THIN AIR	$2.95
☐	56111-2	BEETLE BAILEY: THREE'S A CROWD	$2.95
☐	56068-X	BEETLE BAILEY #4: NOT REVERSE	$1.95
☐	56128-7	BEETLE BAILEY: SEPARATE CHECKS	$3.95
☐	56129-5		Canada $4.95
☐	56092-2	BEETLE BAILEY #8: SURPRISE PACKAGE	$2.50
☐	56093-0		Canada $2.95
☐	56124-4	BEETLE BAILEY: THAT SINKING FEELING	$1.95
☐	56125-2		Canada $2.50

Buy them at your local bookstore or use this handy coupon:
Clip and mail this page with your order.

Publishers Book and Audio Mailing Service
P.O. Box 120159, Staten Island, NY 10312-0004

Please send me the book(s) I have checked above. I am enclosing $_____
(please add $1.25 for the first book, and $.25 for each additional book to cover postage and handling. Send check or money order only — no CODs.)

Name _____

Address _____

City _____ State/Zip _____

Please allow six weeks for delivery. Prices subject to change without notice.